Bluff

www.penguin.co.uk

Also by Francine Toon

Pine

FRANCINE TOON

Bluff

doubleday

TRANSWORLD PUBLISHERS

UK | USA | Canada | Ireland | Australia
India | New Zealand | South Africa

Transworld is part of the Penguin Random House group of companies whose addresses can be found at global.penguinrandomhouse.com.

Penguin Random House UK, One Embassy Gardens,
8 Viaduct Gardens, London SW11 7BW

penguin.co.uk

First published in Great Britain in 2025 by Doubleday
an imprint of Transworld Publishers

001

Copyright © Francine Toon 2025

The moral right of the author has been asserted

This book is a work of fiction and, except in the case of historical fact, any resemblance to actual persons, living or dead, is purely coincidental.

Every effort has been made to obtain the necessary permissions with reference to copyright material, both illustrative and quoted. We apologize for any omissions in this respect and will be pleased to make the appropriate acknowledgements in any future edition.

Penguin Random House values and supports copyright. Copyright fuels creativity, encourages diverse voices, promotes freedom of expression and supports a vibrant culture. Thank you for purchasing an authorized edition of this book and for respecting intellectual property laws by not reproducing, scanning or distributing any part of it by any means without permission. You are supporting authors and enabling Penguin Random House to continue to publish books for everyone. No part of this book may be used or reproduced in any manner for the purpose of training artificial intelligence technologies or systems. In accordance with Article 4(3) of the DSM Directive 2019/790, Penguin Random House expressly reserves this work from the text and data mining exception.

Typeset in 13.5/16.5 pt Sabon MT Pro by Falcon Oast Graphic Art Ltd.
Printed and bound in Great Britain by Clays Ltd, Elcograf S.p.A.

The authorized representative in the EEA is Penguin Random House Ireland, Morrison Chambers, 32 Nassau Street, Dublin D02 YH68

A CIP catalogue record for this book is available from the British Library

ISBN:
9780857527554 (hb)

For my children, who started
life as this novel took shape

Extract from 'Who's Afraid of the Dark?',
Higher English Reflective Essay by Joanie
Sinclair, Hallow's Hill Secondary School, 2012

I have an embarrassing confession to make. I am sixteen years old and I still use night lights. Each evening, when the sun goes down I have to switch three of them on in a particular order. The first is my favourite, a glass rabbit. Its long ears lie against its back and its body shines like a full moon. The star lamp is next, then a toadstool, dotted with light. I know they look childish in my teenage bedroom, alongside my band posters and makeup brushes, but I need them. The ritual started a year ago, when I became paralysed by the dark.

1

Joanie, June 2013

In this corner of Fife, summer nights meant parties on wind-blown beaches. Joanie and her friends would wrap themselves in hoodies and denim jackets, and pretend they weren't cold in the stubborn evening light.

Tonight Joanie's boyfriend, Adam, had told their classmates to gather at the hamlet of Boar's Raik, its bay marked by a bulbous mass of sandstone. School was over and they were celebrating. The rock was known locally as Buddy, looking as it did like a squashed face, watching the beach. The June sky was clear and bright when the first match was lit. As was the ritual, they gathered in a circle around a heap of driftwood, debris and a small collection of textbooks and essays. Joanie scanned the small crowd. One lanky boy was wearing a sheep mask, its plastic face wobbling grotesquely as he danced a jig in the sand. No sign of her best friend, Cara. She was flying to Paris the next morning but had promised to show up.

Her boyfriend had climbed on to a boulder above the fire. 'Here we go, folks!' he yelled, while his friends cheered. He held a branch aloft, then stopped in his tracks. 'Alright Cameron?'

The large, auburn-haired boy had joined the group silently, a carrier-bag of beer in one hand.

'Don't worry,' Adam said, with a cruel smile as he set a branch alight. 'Joanie's safe and sound.'

A couple of people laughed. Joanie cringed. Everyone had seen the video by now. She was lying on the library floor, stage blood smeared on her face, Cameron kneeling over her, looking around in shock, before Joanie and the cameraman had corpsed into laughter.

'It's such a shame, though,' one girl was saying, adding more school work to the fire. 'I thought he was having a pure heart attack.'

'Adam,' Cameron said, from the edge of the circle, 'just get on with it.'

'Alright ya beetroot,' Adam replied, throwing the burning branch into the firewood. King of the year group, he looked older than his eighteen years, his long, fair hair swept into a bun on top of his head.

Joanie knew he hated the video, probably more than Cameron. If he'd had his way she wouldn't so much as smile at another boy.

They were still giddy from Friday's Muck-up Day. Prank phone calls and conga lines and water bombs. Cara had drawn chalk outlines of pupils' bodies in the car park, like a crime scene. One boy had gone from room to room playing Smash Mouth's 'All Star' on the bagpipes. The video prank had been Tatey's idea: Miss Scarlett, in the library, with a candlestick. He had hidden behind a bookcase, then filmed it on his phone.

Joanie believed that she and Tatey had stolen the show. Tatey in particular was already known for playing pranks, usually roping in Joanie and Cameron somehow, but the video had been shared so many times, she imagined the incident would become school lore.

Tiny lights bobbed in the distance, as more teenagers picked their way through the fields and down the steep, sandy steps towards the fire. It was too dark to see whether one of them was Cara. When Adam planned a party, people wanted to come. He had built his reputation by organizing Neuklear Fusion, a local Battle of the Bands. Adam would photograph Joanie for the flyers he made. Last time she had stood on a rock wearing a polka-dot prom dress and sixties eyeliner, a band of artificial roses in her hair. Cameron had posted 'hot' in a comment under the picture. Adam had been furious, even when Joanie had been adamant he had nothing to worry about.

Joanie wore the same flower crown now, standing in skinny jeans. Adam was speaking like a terrible music journalist, proclaiming that a new song could really 'push the musical palette' or that 'The true genius of electroclash has never been fully acknowledged.' Trying to get his attention, she looped her arms round his neck, mid-sentence, and gazed into his eyes, his friends watching.

Soon, other voices grew louder in the burning, salty air. Girls and boys ran in and out of the shadows, playing one last game before they had to grow up.

An elbow nudged her. 'This is the last time we'll ever be together like this,' said her neighbour Graham, squinting into the firelight. He turned to a group of boys, holding his beer aloft.

'Well, thank God for that.' Cara's voice, her face hidden by her tousled red hair, as she reached for a beer in the cool box.

'You made it!' Joanie squeaked, giving Cara a hug. The collar studs of her friend's biker jacket grazed her cheek.

Cara smiled in scarlet lipstick. '*Of course*, babe. Come on. I was stuck at the garage with Doris. The *worst* timing.'

'Doris!' Joanie said, the name of Cara's VW Beetle. The car had been the cornerstone of their social lives that year. If it was ever forensically tested, traces of Joanie's vomit and makeup could probably still be found staining its back seat.

'Doris is an old lady,' Cara said, as they moved away from the boys, to talk in private. 'I haven't even finished packing yet and my flight's *literally* at six a.m.'

'Just pull an all-nighter,' Joanie replied. She didn't want Cara to leave her here. 'Au pair or no pair.' She rummaged in a nearby carrier-bag to fish out two more beers.

'You're kidding,' Cara said, the firelight illuminating her hair. 'My job starts as soon as I arrive. I wouldn't be able to speak French, let alone look after three kids.'

'What's the name of the family again?' Joanie asked. 'The Fourchettes?'

'The Fauchers,' Cara replied.

'Oh! *Excusez-moi, Madame Fourchette,*' Joanie said, in her Advanced Higher French accent. '*Je suis désolée, mais j'aime* – uh – to party.'

'Nailed it,' said Cara, closing her eyes. In the crowd behind them, Cameron was glancing at them nosily. Monsieur Giroud, their French teacher, called him *le Francophile*. She wondered if he was still annoyed with her about the prank.

A couple of hours later, the crowd had swelled. Flames cast long shadows into the late-falling dusk. At some point in the proceedings, Adam, half-cut, jumped off the rocks with a roar. Joanie sighed and picked a strand of hair from her sticky mouth. She noticed some other girls in the crowd wearing flower crowns, cheaper versions. Sometimes classmates copied things she wore. She realized she would miss that, as she took a swig of vodka from a hip flask.

'*Tu me manques*,' Joanie said, making eyes at Cara under her flower crown, as Cara hugged herself for warmth. Her jacket barely covered her flimsy tea-dress.

Her friend shook her head. 'Alright, Lana Del Rey, I've not even gone yet. You'll be off hiking the Rocky Mountains with that guy.' Cara jerked her thumb towards Adam, who was rolling about in the sand like a dog.

'Hmm, more like waiting tables, at least to start,' Joanie replied. The couple would be working at Gassy Jack's, a restaurant run by Adam's uncle in Vancouver. It would make a change from doing shifts in a gift shop. They had planned their itinerary while rearranging Viking helmets and multilingual guidebooks at a local visitor centre for the Isle of Maeyar.

'We're going to talk all the time, OK?' Cara was leaning in close, carefully sober. Her faded red lipstick was smudged. Her fringe almost covered her eyes. 'I hate this, but I have to go now. My dad's insisting on picking me up.'

'Lame!' Joanie shouted into the sky. Her eyes stung and her nose started to run. She leaned into Cara, putting a hand on her friend's shoulder to steady herself. She hadn't eaten much today. 'Aren't you going to say goodbye to Tatey?' she said, too loud, stumbling over a beer can.

Cara rolled her eyes. 'Why would I do that?'

'Because you *looove* him?' Joanie said.

'Go easy on those jazz cigarettes,' said Cara. It was something they said to make each other laugh. Joanie couldn't remember what had started it. 'Hey!' Cara turned and stalked over to Adam, her ankle boots kicking up sand. 'That's me off. Make sure your girlfriend doesn't fall down a ravine, OK?'

'I'll miss you, Nutjob,' replied Adam, going in for a hug.

Cara winked at Joanie over his shoulder. 'Don't get too messy,' she called. They had never spoken about a drunken, tearful night a few weeks ago when Cara had told Joanie she needed to break up with Adam. She was wrong, of course. It had just been a bad argument. All couples had them. Joanie watched her friend disappear up the sand dune, her tangled hair the only spot of brightness in the dusk.

2

Cameron, December 2023

When I finally managed to fall asleep on the late-night train to Edinburgh, I entered a strange, claustrophobic dream. I saw my feet on the stone steps of my old school library. My early-lunch pass was in one hand. When I pushed open the royal blue door, the warm air was infused with the smell of plastic dust jackets.

The library was empty. A couple of books were strewn on the floor. Then I saw her feet, sticking out from one of the aisles. It was my old friend Joanie, lifeless but still beautiful, blood staining her mouth. I fell to my knees, scared to touch her fragile body. Her eyes stared blankly at me. I grabbed her wrist to try and find a pulse, and that was when I noticed she was holding a brass candlestick.

The train jolted me awake as it hit a bump. Fields sped by in the darkness of a Scottish morning. Soon we'd reach Edinburgh and I'd board an early train to Fife. A ghost of my face stared back at me in the glass. It was Christmas Eve and I was almost home.

Extract from 'Who's Afraid of the Dark?' by Joanie Sinclair, 2012

It happened the night Mum and Gary, her partner, visited Judy, my step-granny, Gary's mother. She was excited to meet Elise, her new grandchild. I was invited too, but I didn't want to go. I wanted to spend one night without being woken up by my tiny, colicky sister. I had to promise Mum I wouldn't have a party while they were gone. I also had to promise her that Cara, my best friend, would stay over to keep me company. That day, of all days, Cara started throwing up before she reached my house. Never trust supermarket sushi. I should have told my mother that Cara wasn't coming, but I didn't.

3

Joanie, June 2013

Ignoring Adam, Joanie swivelled towards the huge rock and noticed a head poke out from a long gap in the middle. The person, a girl she recognized from her year, waved a joint towards her, as a question. Joanie looked back at Adam, who was rough-housing his friends, then strode over to join her. Someone, long ago, had carved steps in the middle of the rock, which continued down the other side. Teenagers now filled the space, bringing bravado and uncertainty with them.

'Daniel,' she said, with mock-formality, to the lanky boy who crouched at the top of the steps, rolling another joint one-handed. Everybody called him Tatey. The sheep mask was perched on top of his long, dark hair. If he wasn't an idiot, he would be kind of good-looking. That was what she told Cara, whenever Cara talked about him. Space was created for her to sit next to him. 'I thought you were dead,' someone said, joking about the video in the library.

Tatey shrugged. It wasn't just Muck-up Day: he, Joanie and even Cameron had started pranking each other in primary school. To everyone else at their secondary, Adam included, it didn't even make sense that they were friends. Tatey was an undeniable slacker, Cameron hung out with the geeks in the library, and Joanie was now with the kids who hosted parties. The popular people.

On the rock, a marker pen was passed from person to person to write goodbye messages on clothing. Tatey wrote a whole sentence on the long sleeve of Joanie's surf T-shirt. 'In Heaven,' Tatey wrote, 'all the interesting people are missing.' The pen pressed against her arm. He caught her eye and something passed between them. *Cara*, she thought. *Cara would hate me.*

'Seriously, though.' Another boy was speaking beside them in a rush of smoke. 'Do you ever think there's, like, a simulated universe? The multiverse?'

A girl answered in a voice that set Joanie's teeth on edge: 'I don't believe in the simulation hypothesis. But I've heard there's evidence of a multiverse now.'

'Come again?' Tatey asked.

'They discovered our universe is like a bubble,' the girl continued. 'A bubble that got kind of bruised by other bubbles. It's been proven.' It was Mia speaking; of course it was. A girl who could have been pretty if she had given it some thought. Instead, she had just received the ultimate nerd prize: the school Dux for Sciences. Her name would appear in gold Gothic lettering on a plaque in the assembly hall. Something likely to be filmed by a documentary crew in a few years to come, when she had won the Nobel science award, or whatever it was called.

'Wow, Mia. Go easy on those jazz cigarettes,' called Joanie, her voice cutting sharply through the dark. The bodies around her started huffing with a laughter that grew wild against the roar of the sea.

Mia rose and started to pick her way unsteadily down the stone steps to the beach, turning her back on them all in her awkwardly shaped denim jacket.

Joanie tilted her head up, pretending not to notice. There was something comforting about this tangle of teenage arms and legs, a beached sea monster. The stars shone down through the gap in the rock. Joanie looked up at space for what could have been minutes or hours. Bruised bubbles? She was pretty sure that was bullshit. There were no other worlds. And this one was too frictional to be a simulation.

When Joanie finally crawled out of the nook in the rock, the nervy anxiety that plagued her day to day had stopped, like the absence of white noise. Back on the beach, the wind hit her in the face. The party was in full swing. She scanned the crowd for Adam. Their school was big and word had spread, it was clear. The bonfire towered above them, sending a flurry of embers into the sky, like backwards, hot rain. Stumbling between the dark knots of adolescents, she couldn't find her boyfriend. She didn't recognize many of the shadowy faces. She started to feel sick.

When she moved out to the coolness of the dunes, she spotted Cameron again. He hadn't yet noticed her, as he talked to a girl with a mousy face. Joanie reached up behind him and covered his eyes with her slim, cold hands. 'Guess who?'

She could tell he was blushing in the dark, his shoulders tense. 'I think I know,' he said. 'I think I know who this is.'

She enjoyed this pretend flirting, partly because it clearly irritated the other girl. 'Aw, Cam, you know I'm only teasing you.' She asked him to write on her dove grey T-shirt. He looked even more awkward than usual. The other girl gave him a meaningful look. Joanie had interrupted something.

'We were just talking about uni,' Cameron said hurriedly. His face was pinched. 'I'm studying French. What are you doing again, Joanie? Oh, you're taking a gap year. I forgot.'

'Then I'm doing English at Aberdeen. Why are you speaking like that, Cam?' Joanie asked. 'Have you seen Adam? I can't find him anywhere. The bastard.'

The mention of Adam's name seemed to alarm Cameron further. The girl gave an exasperated look and turned to light a cigarette in the cold Fife wind. Joanie tried to place her in the hierarchical seating arrangements of the school canteen, but came up with nothing. There was a brief moment of silence, filled by the endless shush of the sea.

This was weird. 'So, let me know if you see him . . .' Joanie said, turning to leave.

'Yeah, I know. I know,' the girl said, rubbing the back of her neck. Cameron looked irritated.

'What do you know?' Joanie's speech was slower than normal, numbness creeping in.

'What I mean is, I know Adam,' the girl said.

Joanie did recognize her after all. She was Mia's friend. She had done something different too, a haircut or contact lenses, trying to change herself into a grown-up. At school she sat at the table for the school-newspaper geeks.

'Have you heard of the multiverse?' Joanie asked. The weed was having an effect. She tried to pull herself together. 'Maybe Adam got lost. This party's a lot bigger than *we* had actually planned so I need to find him and . . .' Her voice was hoarse.

Cameron grabbed Joanie's arm tightly. 'Wait a sec, OK?' he said. Cameron knew exactly where her boyfriend was.

'Yeah,' said the girl, reluctantly. 'Hang with us. Whatever.' She was masking something. Joanie looked around her, convinced she was being watched.

'Joanie,' the girl said, her speech slurring. 'I've been trying not to say this. But I've maybe had a few, I admit.' She staggered forward. Joanie stepped back. 'Now school's over, I'll probably never see you again. I just wanna say you were such a bitch.'

'I don't . . . What?' This was so confusing.

'It's all good, like.' It clearly wasn't. The girl's voice was hoarse and shaky. 'No worries. I just wanted to let you know. When you passed us in the corridor or whatever, you'd look at us like we weren't even . . . Like we were pieces of shit.'

'I don't even really know who you *are*,' Joanie said, her voice cracking.

'OK,' Cameron butted in, apologetically. 'This is a party. School's over. Let's try to move on.'

Silence slipped back, like the tide. Joanie watched a distant, illuminated cruise ship and felt a glimmer of sobriety that flickered and went out.

Cameron tried again. 'I'm going to Glasgow and Chloë is . . .' Chloë, that was it. Cameron's voice sank under the weight of whatever he was attempting to hide. Through the fug, she assumed her boyfriend was doing drugs somewhere. It wasn't such a big deal.

'He's out in the dunes, isn't he?' she asked, smiling involuntarily.

Cameron gave a bleak smile. 'OK, on you go,' he said, as Joanie pushed past him.

Away from the light of the party, she lost her footing in the soft, steep sand. Walls of dark grass blocked her way here and there. She switched on the harsh light of her phone's torch and looked back towards the bonfire, where figures were moving like shadow puppets. She had gone too far and was about to turn back to Cameron and Chloë when she heard a gasp. A few strides ahead of her, a hand rose and fell from behind a mound of sand. 'Adam?'

There was silence. Joanie stumbled over in the semi-dark, her torch wavering. Her foot got tangled in material. A sandy denim jacket that looked oddly familiar.

There was a breathy, feminine moan. The male voice hissed, 'Sssh!'

She should have left then, but self-control had vanished.

The male voice was her boyfriend's. She found him crouching among the dunes in his yellow T-shirt and nothing else. His other hand was covering the mouth of a topless girl, who lay beneath him, brown curly hair tangled over her face.

Mia's face.

Joanie had the strange urge to laugh and feel like she wanted to throw up at the same time. 'Fuck you,' she said, and kicked sand at them. She turned and staggered away, like a wounded animal, her legs making the sea grass whisper. As she clambered up the slopes of sand and found the rugged path to the fields, all she could think about was how ugly Mia was. An ugly child. She had been caught in something cruel, dream-like. Her brief eye contact with Adam had made her want to die.

Joanie stopped at the stile on the edge of a field and caught her breath. She could look down from the high bank to the beach. She made out the figures of Cameron and Chloë, huddled, murmuring, clearly looking around for her. They could go fuck themselves too. She had to get far away from this place, if not disappear altogether.

Once she was over the wire fence and walking across the field, she slowed down. By the time she climbed the gate to the main road it was fully dark and the sharp night air stung her hot, swollen eyes. The flower crown had fallen off somewhere along her route. She wiped her eyes and caught the words '*BONNE CHANCE*' scribbled in Cameron's handwriting on her sleeve.

4

Cameron, Christmas Eve 2023

By the time I arrived at the small station, the late-winter sun had finally risen. The air felt cold and clean in my lungs as I hobbled off the Edinburgh train in a small crowd of passengers. I'd reached Waverley at an unholy hour from London, the cramped seating making me feel like the Hunchback of Notre Dame. I hoped the bargain overnight train ticket was worth it. I wasn't quite home yet. Beyond the train tracks at this station, Edenmouth, lay frosted fields and the local military airbase. Its rows of suburban pebble-dashed houses looked incongruous among barbed wire and jet-plane hangars.

I turned towards the footbridge and my heart leaped. Gurning down from the bridge was a man wearing a sheep's head. Terror seized me. The ghoulish mask looked oddly familiar. The lanky body underneath started jigging down the steps.

'Tatey!' I yelled. My breath came out in clouds. He had agreed to give me a lift home, but I wished

I hadn't asked. A family and an elderly couple were walking a few paces ahead of me, unperturbed. They were used to weird students from St Rule. They didn't know that Tatey was too old for this.

'Cab for Morris?' the sheep-man drawled, deadpan. It had been a long time since anyone had addressed me by my surname. His long dark hair was tied in a greasy ponytail.

'St Gregory's wants you back in the flock,' I replied. I hoped one of my fellow passengers would absolve me from this ridiculous behaviour. In London, I wouldn't have cared, but here someone might tell my mum. Or Father Thomas. I was a teacher, for Christ's sake.

Instead of giving him a friendly hug, I wrestled the mask off his sweaty face and, surprising myself, ran up the ramp on the bridge, my suitcase catching my heels. He chased me with unexpected agility, like we were fifteen again. I'd nearly made it to the car park when he shoved me towards a wall. He was actually pretty strong. That, I had forgotten.

'You bastard,' I said, out of breath. 'Merry Christmas.'

A compact, eighties throwback, his old Bessie of a camper van hadn't changed. I was surprised it was still running. He hefted my suitcase into the back, while I folded myself into the passenger seat. The VW's brown, mismatched doors and curtains were weirdly reassuring. 'Your parents not about?' he asked, as I tossed the sheep mask to the back.

'They don't know I'm here,' I said. 'It's a surprise.' The van still smelt of stale weed. He was nothing if not consistent.

Tatey slammed his body behind the wheel and turned on the ignition. Heavy metal blared. He seemed in a particularly good mood. 'You always were a dark horse,' he said, over the noise.

'I'm the whitest horse that ever lived,' I replied, unsure if he could hear me as we rumbled along to the cold coastal road towards St Rule.

My local town, St Rule, had always made me feel like an outsider. As we passed its medieval walls, they looked austere in the frosted light. When people asked me where I was from, I'd prefer to say 'Fife', or even a more general 'Scotland', than mention its name. People tended to associate the place with a kind of pink-shirted, floppy-haired elitism, based on the student population. Or a persistent stereotype, at least. In reality, all sorts of people studied there. Its crumbling architecture provided our small town with a portal to the rest of the world.

The town is known for three centuries-old obsessions: academia, golf and religion. Its three long streets hide secret wynds and chambers, sites of witchcraft and sectarian persecution. Maybe this is why I have always felt a sense of claustrophobia among its libraries and churches and golf courses. Its three paths to enlightenment all require intense focus. The golfer will talk with just as much fervour as the professor or minister about bettering themselves amid the ferocious sea wind.

My shoulders relaxed after we had passed the town and were headed towards Boar's Raik, closer to our tiny village. As the links course turned into fields, I saw the top of the rock we used to call Buddy. In that moment, I could feel cold hands covering my eyes and a girl's voice saying, 'Guess who?'

Whatever happened to Joanie? That teenage girl, playing dead in the library.

Extract from 'Who's Afraid of the Dark?' by Joanie Sinclair, 2012

People often think of teenage girls as difficult, rebellious, sneaky. Hand on heart, while my family left me home alone that night, I was good. I wanted to have a wild party, I wanted to invite a boy over, but I didn't. Instead, I painted my nails the colour of cherries and listened to the haunting melodies of Lana Del Rey. When I was fifteen, the night it happened, I didn't have many friends. All of them were girls. I didn't feel lonely that night, because I had Tinsel to keep me company. She was my cat.

5

Joanie, June 2013

It was close to midnight. Joanie had never walked this stretch of road before, beside the dark expanse of golf course and coastline. She had been driven along it a thousand times, to and from St Rule. Her dying phone calculated that she had to walk a couple of miles to reach the town's suburbs, where she lived. Boys regularly walked double that to get home after parties, even in winter. It was fine.

Her mother would be in bed already, dreaming of church. Either Adam or Cara usually drove Joanie home, he in his blue Fiesta, she in her green Beetle. Joanie remembered Adam's angular face in the torchlight and felt sick. Why on earth would he cheat on her with Mia? It didn't make any sense. They had been together two years, since she was sixteen. At the weekends she would hang out in his musty bedroom, watching him assess demo tracks from various local bands. He would nod to himself thoughtfully, like no one else was in the room.

There was a low, angry rush of a car engine behind her. She willed it to be him, his big arms, and neck that smelt sweetly of sweat. He would try to fix things, magic Mia away. She needed him to. She had a Canadian work visa. There was less than forty-eight hours. The black sea slapped the coastline on the other side of the links.

Fucking Mia. Joanie's face felt numb. Her legs were heavy, like she was trying to walk underwater. A walking joke. She cried harder when the stranger's car passed.

None of it felt real. Like the conversation on the rock, a simulation. Her breath quickened as she cried. Her ribcage tightened. Thoughts were painful, blocking her airways. If she let them in, they would smother her. She wiped her face with the sleeve of her long-sleeved T-shirt, as her pace slowed to a halt. Her breathing was rapid and, as she gasped for air, images tried to wedge their way in. Bare legs in the dark dunes. Caustic eyes in the torchlight. Joanie's chest pulled tighter, bound by an invisible bandage.

In the days after exams, the phrase 'last time' was used by her friends like a meme. 'This is the last time we'll ever drink by the tyre swing,' people would say. 'This is the last time we'll ever go to the petrol station at two a.m.' This was the last time she could call Adam her boyfriend. Her future was slipping through her hands, like sand. Her cheeks were hot and wet. She sank down against a wire fence, sobbing, fighting to breathe.

There was the sound of a car slowing behind her, a soft crunch on the verge. Joanie's spine prickled with the hope that it really was Adam, coming to find her.

'Hey.' A young female voice and a door slamming. 'You OK?' The accent was relaxed, American vocal fry, like someone who had just woken up from a deep sleep.

Joanie was too weak to move. 'Can't . . .' she whispered, eyes screwed tight, hand pressing her chest, '. . . *breathe*.' Then, she was hyperventilating. Her lungs juddered in rapid, mortifying stops and starts.

A tangle of long, surfer-girl hair came into view, then a toothy grin. Large, pretty eyes. 'You're OK,' said the older girl, slowly, crouching next to her, rubbing her back. 'We got you.' A bright flower in the night air.

Joanie opened her mouth but she couldn't make a sound.

'Don't try to talk,' the girl said, her words dragging like the long hem of a dress. 'I think you're having an anxiety attack. I can see it.'

Joanie held the girl's cool hands in silent alarm. Her chest had closed shut. She couldn't force it open. For a terrifying moment, she was sure she was going to die.

'I'm here with you. I know what to do.' The girl had a soothing voice. Her face looked as though it belonged in a stained-glass window. 'Look, over there at the sea,' she said, pointing at the black crush of water to their right. 'That's all you need to do. The waves. Watch them go in and out.' She gave Joanie's hands a squeeze. 'Just watch them.'

Joanie gasped, embarrassingly loudly. A wet sound, like someone who had been drowning. She did as she was told and kept her eyes on the water. Her lungs gasped again. She looked out at Maeyar: a shadowy mass in the water. People went there to spot puffins and walk through its ruined monastery. She and Adam had worked by its ferry's terminus. It took everything to shove those thoughts away.

'I'm here for you. There's no rush,' her new friend said. 'We have all the time in the world.'

Slowly, in the crushing dark, Joanie's breath began to regulate itself.

'This is what I want you to do now,' the girl said. 'Breathe in for four and hold for seven. Got that?'

Joanie met her eyes and, still holding the girl's hands, she followed her instructions.

'OK, now breathe out for eight. This is the four, seven, eight technique. One, two . . .' Her voice was reassuring, even if Joanie struggled to take it all in. 'That's it,' she said. 'In for four . . .'

'Are you OK?' It was a man's voice, English, a little impatient, from the car behind them.

The girl replied as if she had all the time in the world. 'She's doing great.' She looked at Joanie. 'We had a little moment here, didn't we?' The girl was talking to her as if she were a child, but Joanie liked it.

'Are you headed to the town?' the girl asked, in her crouching position, as bangles slid down her tanned arm. Baggy clothes draped her thin frame like sheets.

Joanie nodded. Students called it *the* town. Locals said town.

'Well, we're going that way, if you wanna hop in. I'm Erin. That's David.'

Joanie stood frozen. The fields around her felt vast. She caught her breath and hiccuped. The man leaning out of the window was older, in his thirties, perhaps. Joanie couldn't quite tell. As she rose unsteadily on her feet and walked over, she was able to see that he had a bespectacled, clean-cut appearance, unlike Erin. His strong jaw, his neatly trimmed brown hair, looked oddly familiar.

'I don't know if she trusts us, man,' Erin said, presumably talking to David, then to Joanie, 'I don't like leaving you out here.' She had the wide mouth of a model.

Joanie climbed into the small maroon car, like a stunned animal, and pulled the door with a jolt. Was this OK?

'Take the blanket,' the girl said, as David started

the engine. 'You look cold,' the girl continued. 'What's your name? Do you have panic attacks often?'

This seemed OK. Joanie nodded and said her name with a shaky breath. Even when her relationship had been good with Adam, she would have this shortness of breath. It had started before she had met him, when she was fifteen. The warmer temperature of the car made her shudder. Tears dampened her eyes. On the seat beside her were a couple of rucksacks.

'We're driving home from the Highlands,' the girl said. 'A good thing we were running behind schedule.'

Joanie nodded, focusing on the square black headrest in front of her. There was no radio, unlike Adam's Fiesta, only the persistent hum of the engine.

'So, I was saying earlier,' David's low, affable voice broke the silence, 'that no one *knows* who owned the manuscript in the 1800s.' He was speaking to Erin. 'But I don't know how much it matters. It's irrefutably Aiden of Maeyar and that's really the whole *point* of this paper.'

Maeyar? The gift shop. Maybe that was where she had seen him. Joanie tried to get another look at him, her head foggy. She wondered what university department he worked in. History, by the sound of it.

'Sure, but I'm too tired to talk about this now,' Erin replied, throwing her head back.

'The marginalia is *extraordinary*,' David said.

'You were telling me.' Erin sounded irritated. 'But I don't think *Joanie* will want to hear about it. Joanie, tell me if you're going to puke. You kind of look like you might.'

'I'm fine,' Joanie said, her voice croaky. The woollen blanket felt itchy against her neck. She tried to focus on the road ahead to keep nausea at bay.

'Did I tell you about Aiden's description of the *mergus*?' David asked, unable to contain his enthusiasm. 'It's this wonderful description of a sea bird that lays an egg in a cleft of rock.' He switched on the indicator and took a right turn. '*Aiden of Maeyar: a medieval Attenborough*. That could be another paper. Or a talk! *Mergus*. I'm thinking gannet or guillemot. Can you remember the species we saw on the island? We only went the other week and yet . . .'

Erin shook her head. She was so petite the seat looked almost empty from behind. 'They're pretty similar, right?' she asked. 'Will anyone care?'

'Sounds like a razorbill,' Joanie croaked. She hated that she knew this. From April she had been handing out activity sheets at Maeyar's gift shop to children and bird watchers.

'What's that?' David asked, smiling.

'Razorbills prefer to nest in nooks and crannies,'

said Joanie, in a hoarse version of her work voice. 'Guillemots like steeper parts of the cliffs. Ledges. Maybe gannets do too, but they don't breed on Maeyar.'

David glanced at her in the rear-view mirror, his eyes twinkling behind his glasses. 'And you know this how?'

'Work. Maeyar's visitor centre. I mean I used to. Work there. I'm meant to be leaving for Vancouver in a few days . . .' She trailed off and her chest felt tight again, as she turned to look out of the window.

'Oh, Vancouver's great, Joanie—' Erin began.

Joanie cut her off, her voice quavering. 'Not sure it's happening.'

Erin swivelled her head round, concerned. 'What do you mean?'

'My boyfriend, Adam, he worked with me too. On Maeyar. He was with another girl. At the party, I mean. Just now. I . . .' She couldn't verbalize witnessing the bewildering, drunken sex. She thrust her head into her hands, mumbling, 'I don't know what to do.' She was crying again.

She felt Erin's small hand squeezing her knee.

When Joanie looked up, pushing away tears and makeup and nausea, she saw that they were passing a family pub on the edge of town. She just wanted to go to bed.

'Are you at the university?' David asked gently.

Did she really look like a student? It took a minute

for Joanie to reply. 'No.' She sighed. 'Just finished school.'

'Oh, that makes sense. Forget about Vancouver,' said Erin, with a hint of humour that stung. 'You have to take care of yourself. And you have to be careful,' she went on, 'even out here in this little toy town and this countryside. You don't know who you might meet.' She smiled at Joanie. 'Where shall we drop you?'

Joanie directed her to the house. She lived in a small 1960s semi among a sprawl of identical, suburban houses. They drove right to her faux-wood front door.

'This is a nice area,' Erin said, craning through the windscreen, before Joanie stumbled out. 'I'm so glad we met. Hey, before you go? I work at Hallowed Ground on East Street. The café? You might know us. I'm the manager, actually.' She handed a small card to Joanie. 'So come see me again. If you don't make it to Vancouver, we're looking for a barista.' She smiled. 'At least come and have a free drink.'

'The best peppermint tea in town,' said David.

Joanie looked down at her hands to see she was holding a loyalty card filled with stamps. 'Thank you so much for this.' Joanie waved the card, a wave goodbye. She started to walk up to the path.

'And don't go to Vancouver,' Erin called from the window. 'Stay away from him. It's over.'

She made it sound so simple.

Joanie looked up at the neighbouring houses, worried someone might hear. Graham's family lived across the road. He wouldn't be home yet, thank God. She wondered how far the news of Adam and Mia had travelled. It didn't bear thinking about.

Joanie fumbled with her keys until she heard their berry-coloured car drive away. She didn't want to open the door in front of them. Her house may have looked identical to her neighbours' but inside was a different story.

6

Cameron, Christmas Eve 2023

'Don't park in their drive!' I said, directing Tatey to a layby further up from my parents' house.

'So they think you're spending Christmas with Vanessa and her folks?' Tatey asked, stopping the van with a jerk.

'Man, it's a long story. I'll tell you later,' I said, hoping he might forget about it. 'It' being Vanessa, my former girlfriend. A freelance German translator. Thirty years old. Beautiful. Who was I kidding? My former fiancée. 'Honestly, thank you so much for picking me up. It's great to see you again.'

I wondered what Tatey would be doing now, after I got out of the van. His mum and dad still lived here, in the village of Monypenny, like mine. Did he? Our communication had been spotty over the years. It was nearing nine a.m. and the sky was bright. My legs still ached from spending the night being transported like a battery chicken up the UK's coastline. I wondered if my older sister Kirstin and her small family had arrived home from Edinburgh yet. I wanted to surprise them too, especially my nephew Finn, who was only three.

I looked over at Tatey in the driver's seat. 'So, I would normally invite you in, but my family might be a wee bit overwhelmed,' I said, grimacing. 'I haven't been home for Christmas for a while, there's a toddler. And a dog actually. It's going to be pretty chaotic.'

'Nae bother, man, I get it,' Tatey said, as I undid my seatbelt. 'Wanna come for drinks tonight, though? A few of us are meeting up at Altman's. Christmas Eve and all that.'

'Totally,' I replied, nodding. 'I'm down.' Perhaps because I'd passed the beach at Boar's Raik again, a small part of me hoped I'd see Joanie. If nothing else, I missed the way she used to joke around, talking in stupid voices, teasing me. She always seemed like someone who could be famous one day.

Tatey looked ahead at the cluster of houses and converted barns that made up Monypenny. 'Quite a few folk from school by the sound of it. Need a lift there? Guessing you don't have a car.'

'I'm on my mum's insurance, but no. Yeah, that would be great,' I replied, caught up in thoughts about Christmas and my family as I opened the door, then went round to pull my luggage from the back seat.

'Cool,' Tatey replied, slapping the steering wheel.

'I'll leave you to it. Said I'd make a trifle.' He looked into the rear-view mirror at the non-existent traffic.

'Didn't know I was being driven around by Jamie Oliver,' I said, still leaning into the back seat from the pavement.

'Fuck off,' he said, reaching to push me out of the van.

I staggered back, pointing at the sheep mask on the seat behind him. 'Hope it's not lamb for dinner!'

Tatey shook his head. 'Your sense of humour, man. Cannae say I've missed it.'

My parents lived in a long white cottage, overlooking the sea. On a clear day, you could see the Isle of Maeyar. Today, it was obscured. The waves were low and grey, under a sky like porridge. As I walked up the drive, I noticed that the curtains were drawn at the front of the house. Perhaps my parents weren't up yet. I checked my phone again. My dad's car wasn't there. Maybe they'd gone to pick up Kirstin. I rang the doorbell anyway.

My mother shrieked when she saw me. I caught a look of panic behind her owlish glasses as I reached down to hug her. 'Why didn't you *tell* me you were coming?' she said, flustered.

'Mum?' I asked, with a nervous laugh. 'You OK?' *Nice to see you too*, I thought.

'Oh, Cameron!' she said, a little too loudly, embracing me. '*Cameron!* This is such a surprise.'

Something wasn't right. She looked over her shoulder before ushering me into the hallway. I was greeted by the warm, textured hues of her oil paintings: fish, creels, lighthouses and harbours. She was a former art teacher and local painter. Some of her work had won prizes in East Neuk's annual art festival.

'Why don't you take your bags upstairs and I'll put the kettle on?' she asked, her eyes crinkling with a smile. Maybe I'd been imagining things but I felt strangely disappointed as I took off my trainers on the bottom stair. Where was Dad? This was not the jolly Christmas scene I had expected to find.

Upstairs, my once-turquoise bedroom had been painted a chilly off-white. All my posters, dating back to university, had been taken down and my mum's seashell collection had been arranged on the windowsill. A couple of new paintings adorned the walls. My dad's detective novels lined the bookcase. My parents had certainly mentioned going on a home-improvement spree. It was only now I realized they had been talking about my bedroom.

I dumped my bag on the new beige duvet and heard a noise in the back garden. Footsteps. I peered out of the sash window over the shells. There, walking briskly on the gravel path, from the back garden to the front, was a grey-haired man in a fishing gilet. From above, he looked very like our neighbour, Stuart.

I bolted down the stairs.

BLUFF

'Cameron!' my mum called, urgency in her voice. I found her sitting in the living room, with two mugs of tea and a fire burning in the grate. Sprigs of holly adorned the mantelpiece. I now noticed she was wearing makeup.

'You should have told me, darling!' she said, shaking her head. 'Such a lovely surprise to have you back. This has certainly made our Christmas.'

'Was that Stuart Dunn?' I asked, a little out of breath. I needed to exercise more.

'Oh! Yes . . . well . . . He just needed to borrow the, what's it called, you know, the hedge trimmer. From the shed. I've said if he needs it he's just to go and get it.'

'Uh-huh,' I replied, taking my seat opposite the Christmas tree in the window, which blocked my view of the tool shed. My mum's modest home studio sat further down the garden, partially hidden by a holly bush. I opened my mouth to comment about the time-honoured tradition of Christmas Eve hedge trimming, but thought better of it. Didn't Stuart have more important things to do? As I picked up the tea she had made me, my eyes fell on two used mugs on the coffee table. Clearly he had been inside.

'Where's Dad?' I asked.

'Golf course,' my mother replied, picking up the paper and sipping her tea, as if I'd never left. 'He'll be over the moon you're home.'

I sank back into tartan cushions on the sofa. I'd be pleased to see my dad too. He wasn't one to show his emotions, but I knew it would make him happy. The Christmas tree's familiar decorations caught my eye. Objects that formed part of my early memories. The soothing ice skaters and angels, the red apples, the pom-pom Kirstin made at school.

'And Kirstin?' It had been a while since I had seen my sister.

'Oh, no! Hasn't she told you?' Her voice dropped to a confessional whisper. 'They've got norovirus.'

I stopped myself from swearing. 'Fu—n times. I've got their presents in my bag.'

'Ah, Cammy. She said there's a chance they could be well enough by Boxing Day. I heard it's doing the rounds. We were maybe going to drop something round tomorrow. Wave at Finn through the window. Poor wee lamb. Queensferry Crossing looks a bit dodgy, though,' she muttered, then smirked at me over her reading glasses. 'So! You were planning this all along? I can't *believe* you didn't tell me. You got the bus from the station?'

'Tatey went and got me,' I said. 'I wanted to surprise you.'

'Oh, he's a good lad,' she said, and went back to the paper, picking up a pen for the crossword. Her hair, in its customary bob, was almost white as snow.

In the amiable quiet, I lay down on the sofa and my

back started to feel a bit better. A robin landed on the stone sundial outside. A wren was in the bramble hedge. Somewhere beyond was the sea and London was blissfully further still. It had been too long.

After spending a few minutes doom-scrolling, while my mum asked me for crossword clues, I started to feel hungry. I picked up all the empty mugs and went into the kitchen, looking for some breakfast. The cupboards were filled with the kind of festive food I wasn't sure I was allowed to touch. Cheese straws, biscuit assortments, chocolate oranges, mini slices of Stollen. The room was spotless, apart from two plates sprinkled with crumbs. I placed them and the mugs in the empty dishwasher. Neighbours often popped round. I had nothing to feel suspicious about.

'Do you want a mince pie, Mum?' I shouted hopefully to the living room, taking the box from the cupboard. It was Christmas Eve, after all.

'Oh, no, thank you, I'm fine,' my mum called back. A pause. 'What are we going to do about presents?'

'You sent them down to me, remember?' God, it had felt lonely, receiving that parcel in my empty, decoration-free flat. That was when I had started looking up last-minute train tickets. I had meant to spend the holidays with Vanessa's family in Brighton, eating homemade *Lebkuchen*, baked by her Bavarian mother, but it had all gone horribly wrong.

'Yes,' she called again. 'But you won't have anything to open tomorrow! I'd better go out.'

I heard her mutter something else. 'What was that?' I asked. 'And, Mum, you really don't need to get me anything more, honestly.'

'Och, don't be silly,' she said, entering the kitchen. 'I was asking if Vanessa got her present OK? It should have arrived last week.' The question contained another, hidden, question. Where was my fiancée?

She opened the fridge door, as if to check its packed shelves, when really she was waiting for an answer.

'Oh, yeah, she says a big thank-you,' I replied, lying. Now didn't feel like the time to go into the forensics of all that. Mum liked Vanessa. A lot. I leaned against the kitchen counter and took a bite of an M&S mince pie. 'Are you OK if I go and see some friends for drinks this evening?' I asked. 'Tatey said he can pick me up.'

A vision of Joanie popped into my head. I couldn't help hoping she would be there. When I pictured her face, she was a teenager. Was that creepy? I hadn't seen her since that night on Boar's Raik, now I thought about it. I felt a stab of guilt for how things had ended, even if it was all slightly hazy in my memory. I couldn't imagine how she might look now.

'Right,' my mum said, picking up a William

Morris tote bag that was hanging on the back of the kitchen door. 'I'd better go and see what they've got before the shops close. We need a few things for the house anyway.'

I highly doubted that. 'Mum?' I asked, my mouth full of mincemeat, as she headed to the hallway, bag over the shoulder.

I went out to talk to her, as she wound a hand-knitted scarf around her neck.

'Do you still see the Sinclairs at church?'

'Sinclairs?' she replied. I started to worry my mum was having a senior moment.

'You know, Joanie's family.'

'Oh! Sinclair was the father's name. Her mother's Lynne Byrne. I suppose you were too young to know that. I don't go that often these days, sorry.' She glanced upwards. 'But I'm pretty sure Lynne's not there any more. Well, not *there*, as in church, and, you know, not *all* there. She got a bit . . . funny.' 'Funny' was one of my mother's favourite words.

'Funny?' I asked.

'Oh, you know,' she replied, putting on her woollen patchwork coat and gloves. 'She was always a bit *extreme*, wasn't she? Front row. Holy water. That man Gary as well,' she said, buttoning her coat.

My memories of church were vague, but I could picture the family from behind, kneeling towards the altar. They had a little girl too, Joanie's half-sister.

'What was he, an estate agent?' Mum asked.

'There was something about them that was a bit odd.'

I felt a sharp twinge between my shoulders. Damn that train seat. My head was starting to swim. 'I think I'm going to lie down, Mum,' I said. 'I had such a bad sleep on the way up. My back is killing me.'

'I remember now. It was the house,' my mum said to herself, as she opened the front door to leave.

'What?' I asked. 'What d'you mean, the house?'

'Paracetamol's in the kitchen cupboard, I keep meaning to say.'

'Mum, what about the house?'

'Oh, I can't fully remember,' she said, opening the front door. Then she muttered to herself, 'It did smell very strongly of cats.'

Extract from 'Who's Afraid of the Dark?' by Joanie Sinclair, 2012

We got Tinsel one Christmas from the cat shelter. Her previous owner had thought she was too unlucky, because of her black fur. Tinsel proved to be a shining star. She saw us through some dark family times. Before Mum met Gary, she often had to work long hours so Tinsel and I would spend our afternoons together, after school, the best of friends. My favourite game was trying to find her, crouching under boxes and bags. There were so many places to hide.

7

Joanie, June 2013

Choral music flew through the house like a flock of doves. It was Sunday. Joanie woke up, still wearing her clothes from the party. She blinked at the wall and the room began to tilt. Adam. Mia. Everyone would know by now. Hot nausea washed over her.

To reach the bathroom was an assault course. Boxes of different shapes and sizes were stacked along the narrow landing, while knick-knacks and bags of clothes lay strewn on the floor. It had been like this since Joanie was little and her parents had parted ways. 'Elise likes it,' was her mother's latest excuse. 'There's lots for her to play with.' In truth, the house was no place for a toddler.

Joanie locked herself in the bathroom and threw up in one big lurch. Tears ran down her cheeks. She screwed up her eyes and concentrated on the CD that was playing downstairs: 'Ave Maria'. Now and again she would hear the sounds of her family getting ready for church: shuffling and muted voices.

The cat whining for breakfast. Her two-year-old sister Elise whining because she didn't want to eat her breakfast. After a few minutes, the nausea began to ease and the Feeling descended. The familiar feeling of wanting to hurt herself. She crouched by the bath, resting her forehead on its cold edge and held off the Feeling as long as she could. She had disgusted Adam, because she was a disgusting, stupid girl. She forced her nails down the inside of her arms, making deep pink tracks. She cried in gasps, like she was trying to keep her head above water.

'Joanie?' her mother called, from the bottom of the stairs. 'We're leaving soon.'

Why couldn't she be left alone? They would be in their jackets already. Joanie pushed her way to her bedroom, her hands feeling her way past the boxes of crap, her feet kicking away bags, nearly tripping her over. She tossed herself on to her bed and curled up in a ball, crying. It was over. Nothing mattered any more. He didn't love her. Everything, every plan, had drained out of her life. As she cried, her breathing became ragged, until it started to feel independent from her body.

Light footsteps pummelled up the stairs.

'Oh, for goodness' sake!' Her mother's bird-like frame stood in the doorway. She was wearing a severe shift dress that would have looked more fitting for an office. Somehow, even though the house was teeming with junk, her mother never had a hair out of place. 'What's happened now? Come on. We're going to be late.' She tugged Joanie's arm to make her sit up. Her nails dug in. She did not understand.

'Don't touch me.' Joanie pushed the words out as her breath zigzagged from her lungs. It was the same as last night when the girl had held her hand. Erin. Her mother's icy stare made her feel stupid. 'Mum . . . I can't . . .' The walls, all the stuff in the house, she felt they were going to close in and bury her. The image of Erin was becoming fuzzier. Her breathing was becoming more laboured. The bandage round her ribs was pulling tight.

The silhouette of the Isle of Maeyar came back to her. *Four, seven, eight*, Erin had said. *Breathe in for four, hold for seven, out for eight.*

'I don't have time for this,' her mother muttered, pulling out clothes and putting them next to her on the bed. 'Don't think we're leaving you here, madam.'

Joanie closed her eyes and tried to tame her breath, like a wild horse. *Four.* She managed two. *Seven.* She held for two. She made an embarrassing rasp.

Her mother tutted, turning to leave. 'You've got two minutes.'

Joanie clung to the numbers Erin had spoken and her breath started to settle. She gripped the bedspread. She was going to be OK. She wasn't going to die.

Tinsel jumped up to greet her, purring. Joanie gently stroked the black fur, until her lungs began to regulate themselves.

Her mother and Gary were waiting in the car by the time Joanie was downstairs. Joanie observed them numbly. Her mother seemed to be growing thinner by the week and older than her years. Gary was in his fifties but still had the round-cheeked look of a sulky toddler. Elise, now buckled into her car seat, was waving a board book. Joanie smiled mechanically at her baby sister, as she strapped in next to her. She would move her body from A to B, shutting out any errant feelings, and figure out the rest later.

'We're going to be late,' her mother said. 'I've had enough of your drama.'

Joanie pretended she hadn't heard.

They were looking forward to her leaving. She could have told them, there and then, about Adam, but there was a strong chance that their reaction would make things worse and she would start crying all over again.

Instead, Joanie fixed her eyes on the passing scenery and let her mind fly up into the trees like a bird. *Four, seven, eight*, she breathed softly.

Church was a marble lung, decorated with saints and stars. As they entered, she saw Tatey's mother and his two sisters, kneeling in one of the back pews, their black hair falling over their faces as they bowed their heads in prayer. Tatey hadn't come back here since he had been in trouble. Most Sundays Joanie's family were the first to arrive, but today they had to pass the rest of the congregation who were whispering, praying, fiddling with their Order of Mass, as the first notes of the organ started.

'In the name of the Father, the Son and the Holy Spirit, amen,' Father Thomas declared, making the sign of the cross. He was tall and grey, in cream robes. Joanie's hand moved as if by its own volition, crossing her body in answer. As it did so, she glanced around, hoping to spot Cameron on the other side of the aisle. He should have told her something was going on last night. Had he been annoyed with her about the prank in the library?

When it came time for Joanie to kneel on the embroidered hassock in front of her, a voice inside her head said, *Adam, Adam, Adam*, like the hammering of her heart. Maybe there was a way to make sense of this. *O Lamb of God*, the choir sang gently, *thou takest away the sins of the world, have mercy upon us.*

During Father Thomas's homily, about simple acts of compassion, tears started to trickle down Joanie's face. She couldn't stop them, didn't know what was happening. She was simply crying, her palms together, heart pierced by tiny swords. The priest would see her. Wasn't this sort of the point, though? To feel compassion, sadness, grief, guilt. Her mother shifted uncomfortably in her pew.

Wiping tears away, Joanie croaked through the hymns and performed each ritual as if in a trance. Her mother believed that the more Joanie went to mass, the easier she would lose her anxious habits. It wasn't entirely untrue. Something about going through each motion, each muscle memory, helped. Genuflecting in the aisle, bowing towards the smoking thurible, taking communion, they were all actions that focused the body and purified the mind. Devotion put an end to suffering.

Later, when Father Thomas said, 'Let us offer each other a sign of peace,' Joanie could not see Cameron, just his parents and sister Kirstin, as she turned to shake hands with the people behind her, her eyes darting to each corner of the nave. He must be hungover. Tatey had essentially been banned. *Adam and I are done*, Joanie texted Cara, half hiding the phone up her sleeve. *Feel like shit. He hasn't even messaged me.*

By the end of the service, the tears were still coming. Her mother put an arm round her shoulders to hurry her out of the doorway, where Father Thomas was waiting to greet them. 'It happens,' he said, smiling kindly as they passed. 'It happens.'

Maybe she should become a nun, lock herself away in an abbey and never have to deal with boys again. Normally, after the service, her family went to the church hall, where they would be drinking tea and diluting juice. Instead, to Joanie's relief, her mother ushered them into the car. They had somewhere special to go today, she said tightly. 'So cheer up a bit.'

'I'm sorry,' said Joanie, putting her head into her hands in the back seat next to Elise. No one seemed to notice. *What's up?* Cara had texted back, but Joanie couldn't bring herself to reply. She felt like a small child. Joanie repeated herself, louder, and her mother shrugged, which made her feel worse. This was just a shock. She couldn't refund her flight. She couldn't sit next to Adam for eleven hours in a confined space. She couldn't go to Canada without a job. Surely he didn't want to be with her either. If he apologized, there was a sliver of possibility that she could board the aeroplane.

As they set off in the car, Joanie picked at the frayed sleeve of her jacket until she felt sick. She watched people coming out of other churches in the town. The streets were busy. Religion had created St Rule and religion still nourished it.

Even university students had somewhere to be on a Sunday morning. Joanie caught a glimpse of them, walking in a crocodile out of the university chapel, in their famous magenta gowns. As was ancient tradition, they were on their way to the cobbled town harbour, to process back and forth along the grey stone arm that stretched out to sea.

Gary pulled up outside Giovanni's, the family restaurant they always went to on special occasions. He got out without looking at any of them, his lips pouting downwards.

'Hope you're feeling better,' Joanie's mother said flatly, as her small, bony fingers fiddled with Elise's car seat. It wasn't a question. 'We wanted to take you here as a surprise.'

An awful realization dawned. This was a farewell meal in honour of Joanie's year in Canada, planned in advance. She should have told her mother what had happened, back at the house. The worst thing she could do was cry again.

They took their seats at a table spread with a red checked tablecloth, while black-and-white photographs of Italian actors stared down at them. The whole place was cluttered with framed newspaper clippings and art-nouveau posters for Campari and mopeds. Joanie examined the menu intently, tapping her fingers on the table. Nothing had changed since the previous time she had been there, or the twenty before that. 'Order whatever you like,' Gary said emotionlessly. Her mother looked at him fondly. He meant something cheap to middling.

The truth bubbled up inside Joanie and she felt her mouth go dry. 'I've got to cancel the flight.'

'What do you mean? What's happened?' her mother asked, her hand touching her earring, a small Celtic cross.

'Adam was with another girl,' Joanie muttered, looking down at the table. She couldn't say anything more graphic. Her mother believed Adam had never gone further than to kiss Joanie, let alone anyone else.

'*Was what?*' her mother replied. 'I thought he dropped you off last night. Are you sure?'

Was she *sure*? The question stung with a particular kind of parental acid as the sex scene from the previous night flickered in her memory.

Joanie sniffed. 'Obviously.'

Her mother carried on: 'I can't believe he would do that.'

'So. Yeah.' Joanie wiped away a tear forcefully. 'I'm pretty upset. As you can see.'

Gary was staring, heavy-lidded, into the distance, as he did whenever things became heated.

'That's knocked me for six,' her mother continued, looking around the room as if Adam might appear at any moment. 'He's such a nice boy. I really can't believe he would do something like that. You're so good together. And what about the trip? You have everything ready. Are you sure you can't—'

'*Mum.*' Joanie glared.

'OK. No need to take that tone,' said Gary. A tiny pool of spittle had gathered at one side of his mouth. 'Your mother's only trying to help. So, let's get this straight: you're saying you're not going to take the flight with Adam.' He was no doubt thinking the meal was a waste of money.

'No. I can't. Not when he was shagging another girl.' She wanted to walk out of the restaurant without looking back.

'Joan. For *Heaven's* sake,' her mother said. 'Language.'

'Elise won't understand me,' Joanie replied, knowing this wasn't the point. Her little sister was watching her, a kids' menu crayon in each hand. She swivelled her head, looking around. The restaurant was filling with other families, here for a Sunday treat. A waiter caught Joanie's eye from the other side of the room and started to stride towards them. He was a boy from school, in the year below. Joanie didn't know his name. Had he been at the party? Did he know what had happened to her?

'Anyway,' her mother continued, 'let's see. You never know.'

Had her mother misheard what she had said? Joanie studied the empty glass on her table. She heard the boy clear his throat behind her left shoulder.

'Two more minutes, please,' her mother said briskly, before the waiter could open his mouth. 'I'd hold off on cancelling anything for now,' her mother continued. 'I'm sure it'll all come out in the wash.'

This reaction was even worse than Joanie had expected. It was true that they liked Adam very much and thought she was 'difficult' to live with, but this was ridiculous. A betrayal of the highest order. Adam's infidelity was too inconvenient to be acknowledged.

'Mum,' Joanie said, again, 'this is real. It's, like, *tomorrow*. I'm not going.'

'Well!' her mother replied, exasperated. 'I don't know what you want us to say! What now, then? *What now?*' There was a histrionic note in her voice, almost sarcastic, like she was mocking Joanie.

'I need to think about it,' Joanie said. She was starting to zone out.

'Of course, of course,' Gary said, wiping his mouth with a napkin. 'So, on the bright side, this isn't a goodbye meal after all, eh?'

Joanie smiled weakly. It would have taken a lot for him to say that.

8

Cameron, Christmas Eve 2023

'Morris!' It had been a couple of years, but I'd recognize Graham Donaldson's voice anywhere. Guys from home were the only people who called me by my surname. Tonight it was booming across Altman's, our favourite pub, like the past ten years hadn't happened. I saw him now with a large group of people from school, standing in one corner of the dim cellar bar. A Christmas Eve tradition.

'Donaldson!' I replied, making the international gesture for 'I'll get you a pint.'

Tatey went straight to one of the tables and started joking with a couple of guys, who were sitting with the ease of regulars. I was happy to delay talking to anyone by going to the bar.

On the way over, the streets of St Rule had looked different. There were even more preppy clothing boutiques, decorated with holly. Artisanal gin and Celtic jewellery glistened in the shop windows, framed by baubles. The twinkling Christmas lights had looked bigger and brighter than in years past. Despite my earlier feelings, seeing the town in all its festive glory was a bit like being hugged by a favourite aunt at Christmas. I *had* missed this place. Altman's Bar, with its wood-panelled walls, felt as worn and welcoming as an old pair of slippers. Upstairs by the entrance, a girl with an acoustic guitar was playing a folksy rendition of 'Santa Baby'. Her voice reverberated through the ceiling above us, taking me back to the gigs we used to go to as teenagers.

Not much had changed about the place. Among the dartboards, beer mats and tinsel trod the spectres of our adolescence. As I brought the drinks to the table, I noticed small differences in the faces of my former classmates: a bit of weight gained, some hair lost. I didn't recognize a couple of the girls at first – they looked so, well, sophisticated now. God, there was Chloë. We had got off together, years ago, at the party at Boar's Raik. There was awkward kissing. I got sand in my mouth. I remembered waking up early on the Sunday morning at her house and having to sneak out before her family woke up. There had been a bit of explaining to do once my parents had come back from church too.

Chloë and I had gone out for a few months. It had been hard to keep seeing her, once I started a summer job at a pub in Dundee, mostly staying with my aunt and uncle. As the summer came to an end and I packed my bags for uni, I had decided to call it off. Maybe that had been mean, but she hadn't seemed particularly upset. She had been busy, trying to get experience in media, mostly online magazines.

We had bumped into each other a few times since then, but I never knew what to say to her. I looked at her now. I was pleased to know that her hard work had paid off. She was a journalist and had written for some major newspapers. I can't say I didn't keep a look out for her byline. The women she was sitting with exuded the kind of glossy confidence that suggested boardrooms and spin classes. When she looked up, I turned the other way. What did I look like to Chloë and the other girls from my year? Could they tell I was a French teacher? That I had spent the past seven years in London? I probably seemed out of shape. Maybe Chloë had already looked me up too.

'Bring it in, big man,' Graham Donaldson said, in his gruff monotone, hugging me and taking a pint out of my hand at the same time. He worked in recruitment now. Or perhaps it was consulting. I had forgotten. He had bulked up, for sure, and his skin had a sun-bed hue. Only he could have come out of the post-pandemic years looking better than before.

Graham told me about the recent golf championship at St Rule and I told him about the journey up.

He had a way of talking in which his mouth barely moved. I scanned the room, privately wishing that Joanie would bounce in.

'So have you and Vanessa set a date yet?' Graham asked abruptly.

My blood ran cold. 'Not yet, man, a lot going on,' I said, scratching my head. It wasn't a lie, just an omission of the truth, which was easier right now. My tone made it clear I didn't want to talk about it, but he carried on, asking if we would be getting married in St Rule.

'Ach, no, I don't think that's on the cards,' I said, running my hand through my hair.

It was vague enough to be true. This wasn't the place to get into it. I didn't want to kill the festive buzz.

An American guy in a puffer jacket was talking loudly beside me. 'The sound in here is *di*abolical. The acoustics . . . *Hey*.' He caught my eye. 'Cameron Morris! Long time no see.'

I looked again. His blond hair was short and he had a beard, but he was unmistakably my former classmate and adversary. Adam. 'Oh, my *God*. I didn't recognize you,' I said.

He laughed his old, generous laugh. 'Time hasn't been kind,' he said. What a douche.

'That's not what I meant,' I replied. He was as good-looking as ever. 'I haven't seen you since . . .' Since we were eighteen and he was trying to humiliate me at that beach party. I could still see his friends' faces in the firelight. '... school. You sound so American,' was all I could think to say.

'Canadian. I work in Vancouver now,' he said, laughing that laugh, like someone who hunted moose for sport. 'Software. It's been a minute.'

It's been a minute. More like a decade. Did he even remember what a dick he'd been? He didn't show any sign of it.

I took a gulp of beer. 'You still see Joanie?' I asked, trying not to sound too eager. He used to hate us being friends. Then I remembered. He'd got off with some other girl at that beach party. I remembered Joanie running off into the dunes, the soft slopes making her stumble. Maybe I went after her. The image was unclear. Even if Joanie *was* in town, there would be no way she'd want to come here.

He crossed his bulky arms. 'No, I don't see Joanie any more. *You?*'

He knew I didn't. I could tell by the way he was looking at me.

'It's been a minute,' I said, and took another gulp of my beer.

'Right.' He zipped up his jacket and clapped me on the back, definitively. 'I'm heading off, but I hope you have a great Christmas.'

'Same,' I said. I hoped his Christmas was shit. With a self-important salute to his loyal fans, he made for the staircase and my eyes swivelled around the pub once again.

Tatey was playing darts with some girl. Graham was buying me a pint. It was probably a good thing Joanie hadn't shown up.

I started to make my way back to the bar when I felt two slim hands on my shoulders. 'Hey,' a voice said in my ear.

I turned.

It was someone else. A woman with dark curly hair. Her name was on the tip of my tongue. All I managed to recall was her social-media handle: @BookDragon. Somehow that had replaced her real name in my head. From her posts over the years, I knew that she had lived in Bristol, moved back here, worked in a bookshop and liked wild swimming. Myra? What was I thinking? No sane parent would call their daughter Myra post-1965.

'I hope I wasn't interrupting anything,' she said. Her eyes, now that I noticed them, were deep and brown. She wasn't wearing much makeup, but she didn't need to. If she wasn't part of this reunion class, I would have thought she was a few years younger than me.

'No, no, just catching up,' I said, trying to sound friendly.

'About Joanie,' she replied, giving me a look I couldn't quite fathom. Had she been eavesdropping?

'Are you drinking mulled wine?' I asked.

She looked a little forlorn. 'I remember you were friends. I haven't seen Joanie for a long time and . . .' she looked around her '. . . it's actually a little concerning.'

'What do you mean?' I asked.

'Well, I—'

'Mia!' Tatey butted in. Joanie's friend, Cara, I saw now, was standing further behind him, looking away, as if trying to find someone better to talk to. I nodded, but she seemed not to see me.

Mia. Of course. I remembered now that she'd spent a lot of time studying, wearing bigger, chunkier glasses than those she had on now.

'Bet you or Cameron will know this one,' Tatey said to her. 'Cameron, does "bi-weekly" mean once every two weeks or twice a week?' It was a classic Tatey non sequitur. He was the kind of guy you wanted on a pub quiz.

'Excuse me a sec,' said Mia, putting her hand on my back as she moved away. She barely looked at Tatey or Cara. I felt as though I was missing something.

My thoughts scrambled. Cara had always been with Joanie, driving around in her old car. 'Both?' I asked.

'How can it be both?' Cara asked. '"Bi-weekly" means twice a week.'

'Well, what do you call *every two weeks*, then?' asked Tatey.

'Fortnightly,' replied Cara, 'Stop being such a numpty.' I had a memory of Cara and Joanie, stargazing on the bonnet of the little green car. They had given it a funny old lady's name. Deirdre perhaps. Or Dorothy.

'Oh, *ho-ho-ho*. "Fortnightly", is it? Is that how we talk in Edinburgh, now?'

God, Tatey was a charming bastard when he wanted to be. I had forgotten that side of him.

'Look, St Rule is way posher than Edinburgh, anyway,' replied Cara.

'I'm not from St Rule,' Tatey replied. Here we go.

I pivoted round to find Graham – surely he had bought me that drink by now. When I went over to the bar, I saw Mia again, smiling.

'What are you up to, these days?' I asked.

'I was going to ask you the same thing,' she said. She had a way of speaking that put me at ease. 'I came back here for a PhD.'

'Let me guess,' I said, trying to sound like Tatey and failing. 'Biology?'

She looked taken aback. 'Wait, how did you . . .? Marine biology.'

'Aha!' I said, triumphant. A memory surfaced. 'I remember once you did this project on eels. You told me about it in the library. Or was it seals?' I wished I could remember these little details. And act a little less keen.

Mia smiled. 'Probably both. One likes eating the

other. I can't believe you remember that . . . I actually did maths for my undergrad degree.'

That was it: she'd got the Dux for Sciences. 'Well, you were good at maths too.' Was I flirting?

She smiled. 'You should have told me I preferred seals.' Was this flirting?

'A seal of approval.' OK, I ruined it. Kill me now.

'And you?' She was playing with her corkscrew hair, seemingly unrepelled. Just then Chloë passed by, studiously ignoring us, and Mia gave a little wave.

A cold chill ran down my spine. Mia had been with Adam that night. The reason Joanie had run off. Damn it.

'Me? Er, I'm a French teacher,' I said, looking around. Where had Donaldson gone? He'd probably drunk the pint himself by now. 'I'm looking for Donalds—'

'Here you are, Morris,' Donaldson said, pushing the cold, full glass into my hand. My one excuse to exit this conversation.

'It's getting late,' said Mia, to my relief. 'I've gotta be up early tomorrow.'

'Open those presents from Santa,' said Donaldson, with the kind of squint that belonged in a blizzard.

'Ha! Something like that.' Mia looked up at me. 'Hope to see you again.'

A wave of exhaustion swept over me. I was done in. I needed to get back to Tatey, my ride home.

'Hey!' Tatey said, almost shouting in my ear. The pub had become rowdier. 'How about we swing by midnight mass? "Ding dong merrily on high"!' I could tell from his voice that he'd had a few beers.

'It's – I'm gonna get a taxi,' I shouted back, looking at him and then Donaldson. 'Got no sleep on the way up.'

'Sure,' replied Donaldson. 'I'm offski. Maybe we get in nine holes before you leave or somethin'.' I wondered if he had ever tried ventriloquism. An image of him talking to Joanie, with the same indiscernible expression, came back to me from some dark recess. Donaldson and I had been talking at the party, then I had gone off with Chloë, hopeful. But where was Joanie now? I had never seen her again. Not even at church.

I checked my phone. I could hold up for a couple more hours. 'Actually, Tatey, I'll come with you.'

Extract from 'Who's Afraid of the Dark?' by Joanie Sinclair, 2012

The night in question, I lay on my bed watching my Mean Girls *DVD on the small pink TV in one corner of the room.* Mean Girls *is one of my favourite films. I have watched it perhaps fifty, even a hundred times. The glow of the TV illuminated my starry duvet while Cady and her friends danced across the screen to 'Jingle Bell Rock'. I imagine them now, keeping watch over me, like guardian angels in mini dresses. At some point during the film, maybe during the Mathlete state final, I fell asleep.*

9

Joanie, June 2013

On one of the residential roads from her house, Joanie pulled her phone out of her pocket. Her brain seemed hardwired to want it, no matter what she did. People from school would be talking about her. She knew some girls would be happy to see her brought down a peg or two. There were a couple of messages from Cara about the break-up. One was sympathetic, doused in heart emojis, followed by a cute gif. The next was rousingly motivational, telling Joanie how much better she was without Adam. He had never been good enough for her anyway. It certainly didn't seem true, but her friend's support meant a lot.

Then there was a text from her neighbour, Graham Donaldson, asking if she had arrived home safe from the party. That was sweet of him. He looked out for her now and again. She sent a couple of quick replies, then stuffed her phone back into her pocket. She needed to concentrate on where she was going.

Walking to St Rule's Old Town meant navigating the maze of her sprawling housing estate. Cul-de-sacs repeated again and again, homes that were replicas of her own. Perhaps she would have been able to walk around them blindfolded, touching their parallel kitchen-diners and bedrooms. She often thought this symmetry would be pretty beneficial to burglars. If you'd broken into one, you could raid them all.

The day was soundless. A pigeon flew into the old doocot as she approached, a medieval throwback in beige suburbia. It would take twenty minutes to walk from here, the southern suburbs of St Rule, to the centre of town. It was Monday morning and most people, including her mother and Gary, had left for work. The clean, empty roads were designed for family cars and kids' bicycles, not teenage girls on long, anxious walks. She shuddered. Adam would be picking up his backpack off a carousel at Vancouver airport right now. Not that he had spoken to her. Why hadn't he? Her hand touched her phone again.

Many of the neat suburban gardens had their own cherry trees. They had been donated in the 1970s by a benevolent Japanese businessman, or so legend had it. They had bloomed pink each March, but if you looked up close a disease had started to creep in, deforming their trunks.

Compulsively, Joanie grabbed the phone out of her pocket again and swiped at the screen, furious with herself. A list of notifications showed a few nosy classmates, asking if she was OK. She pushed them away, one by one.

She had now reached the Mill Braes, a public footpath that led into town. Maybe she should post a hot selfie, to show everyone she was fine. She held up her camera and the face that stared back at her was tired and pale.

Another message flashed up from Tatey. *In town – you about?*

She used to tell people Tatey and Cameron were like brothers to her, but they weren't, not really. They had simply grown up at the same church. An embarrassing, semi-secret fact. To Tatey, from Monypenny, Joanie lived 'in town'. What had he written on her sleeve? *In Heaven, all the interesting people are missing.* What did that mean? She put her phone back into her pocket.

When they had exchanged a look at the beach party, she had felt a secret thrill that was almost like fear. It was the same feeling when he had asked her to play dead in the library, knowing Cameron was about to start his monitor duty. He had thought that Cameron was easy to fool.

Joanie jabbed at her phone again, once she had reached the crenellated town walls. Did Erin's café even exist? There was no search listing for Hallowed Ground, no map pin, no social media, no reviews.

Nevertheless, she continued through the arch into the Old Town, hoping to find it if she walked up East Street.

While it was true that St Rule thrived on ceremony and tradition, its existence was also sustained by an economy of coffee houses, gloomy pubs and quaint bookshops. The places, in other words, where people spent their time between communion, lectures and the golf course. As Joanie headed towards the twin steeples of the ruined cathedral, the muggy air pressed at her temples and the summer rain spat down.

The rain was beginning to fall faster when she saw Tatey's lanky figure shuffling along the pavement. He raised a hand solemnly, in greeting.

'What are you doing up so early?' she asked, instinctively looking around for the clapped-out van he drove. He sometimes transported bands' equipment in the back, driving to and from local gigs, but Adam had always seemed intensely irritated by him. *He looks like he sleeps in that van*, Adam would say. *It's disgusting.*

'Stuff,' Tatey said. 'Y'know.' He was looking at her differently.

'Just saw you texted me,' Joanie said.

'Yeah. I wondered if you wanted to hang out.' He didn't break eye contact.

'Maybe later,' said Joanie, without really thinking about it. 'Have you heard of a café called Hallowed

Ground? I'm trying to find it. I've got to go there for a potential job thing.'

'Gnarly,' replied Tatey, with an expression she couldn't quite read. She appreciated that he wasn't mentioning the Adam Situation, as she now thought of it.

He cocked his head thoughtfully. 'I think it's part of the Divinity School.'

She felt a pang of uncertainty. The Divinity School. Erin had been so friendly. Was this something evangelical? One of those youth-recruitment drives, like the Jesus Bus that parked outside school and handed out plastic crucifixes? She wouldn't know unless she tried.

'Catch you later,' said Tatey, as she made her way past him.

The Divinity Quad was beautiful in the light summer rain. In its centre stood a wizened tree with a plaque, certifying its eighteenth-century origins. Its spindly branches spread towards any passing students like a bony embrace.

At first, she couldn't see anything other than the building: a patchwork of stone and ornate windows along each side of a slick, verdant square. Each window consisted of three long rectangles and within each were rows of smaller white ones. When Joanie tried to look at them all together, it was dizzying. The walls of the building were punctuated with architectural flourishes, such as weathered staircases, stone-crested doors, dinky turrets and curling ornamentation, green with age. As her eyes ran along the next wall, she spotted a small sign above a door in the corner that read HALLOWED GROUND in the university's antiquated font.

She approached carefully along the glistening gravel path, past the climbing roses, wet with raindrops. The windows either side looked darker than the others. They were obscured now, she saw, by large arrangements of dried flowers, corn stalks and feathery sprays of deep yellow and orange. Underneath the sign, the door was plastered with damp posters for yoga and meditation.

At that moment, a tall man pushed his way out of the door, carrying a pile of books. Joanie stood aside to let him by, then caught the door as it swung shut. As his tweed jacket brushed past her, she realized it was the academic in tortoiseshell glasses who had been in the car with Erin.

She watched his face change in recognition and surprise. Yes, she was the messy, crying girl they had picked up on the drive home. The one who knew about birds.

'Ah,' he said. 'Hunting down a peppermint tea!'

'I've heard they're good,' she said, making him smile, as he staggered off under the weight of his reading list, his head bowed in the rain.

As Joanie pushed open the door, there was a

faint smell of must, as though she were walking into a library. Unexpected light filled her eyes, from Gothic windows that sat high in the opposite wall. Bookshelves lined the edges, but the rest of the space was given over to second-hand tables and chairs, a large counter with an espresso machine, and house plants of different shapes and sizes.

Joanie's eyes scanned across the tables to the handful of academics who were drinking cups of tea and reading. She couldn't see Erin, so she walked up to the man at the counter. He smiled at her, tall and of South Asian heritage, a piercing on one side of his lower lip. His dark, unruly hair was just long enough to tuck behind his ears.

'What does this get me?' Joanie asked, placing the card in front of him.

'A drink? Whatever you want.' There was a lilt to his voice that confirmed to Joanie he was probably an international student, maybe even a postgraduate. It was hard to tell, but he still looked disconcertingly similar to her in age. The students of St Rule had always seemed so much older and more sophisticated, living hidden lives behind the university's high walls, before jetting back to different parts of the world. Now she was the age of the incoming freshers, an interloper.

Rain began to batter the window above them. There was no menu behind the counter. 'What kind of coffees do you have?'

'We do normal coffee, of course, the usual, but really, we specialize in herbal teas. Many different kinds.' He slid a small menu towards her, the sleeve of his jumper falling over his hand. There were glass cylinders behind him, filled with the dark fragments of dried leaves and flowers. The air smelt faintly of peppermint.

Joanie scanned the list. 'I'll have a Cosmic Chamomile. You guys are new?' she asked, looking at the shelves lined with battered paperbacks.

'We opened last year,' he said. 'This used to be part of the Divinity Library. The university figured they needed to make more money.' He sighed. She watched as he began to prepare the drink, scooping out dried leaves from the clear container. 'Low on staff today,' he said. 'I'll bring it over. We just ask that people keep the space a digital-free zone. No phones or laptops if you can. Cheers.'

She took a seat at an empty table, unsure if this was all there was to Erin's offer. She would take advantage of what she could. She wished she had known about this place earlier. It had a laid-back studenty charm. Her friends all wanted to go to shiny, minimalist establishments for people who liked flat whites, MacBooks and selfies.

Turning off her phone felt like pulling down a small shutter on the world. She saw a large painting to her right. A cottage on a steep rocky outcrop that plunged down to the waves. Its shoreline was dotted with flowers.

At that moment, two girls with backpacks entered, having a conversation in another language, soaked from the rain. The windows had steamed up. They peeled off their shoes and jumpers and curled up on a threadbare sofa, hair sticking to their faces.

There was still no sign of Erin. Perhaps it was her day off. Joanie browsed the bookshelves, which held paperbacks that looked like they had been pillaged from the local charity shops. They were divided into a hotchpotch of different sections. *Gardening, Yoga, Scottish History*. She ran her finger over the spines of the latter shelf and selected a title at random: *A Life of a Saint: the real story of St Rule*.

She sat down at a table and scanned the first page self-consciously.

St Rule, as the legend goes, set sail from Greece around 300 AD, accompanied by several virgins. According to varying accounts, Rule was either shipwrecked or told by an angel to stop intentionally on the shores of Fife at a Pictish settlement . . .

Someone was standing close to her chair. Joanie raised her head, smelling the chamomile tea.

'You came,' said Erin, holding the cup in both hands, her face like a pale, polished pebble. 'I just arrived. The rain is ridiculous today. Here you go. How are you feeling?'

'I'm OK.' Joanie felt ashamed of her drunken

behaviour in the car. 'Thank you so much for the tea.'

'Oh, of course.' Erin stretched out her hands, in her cropped green T-shirt. 'I love your outfit by the way.'

'Oh, thanks, same,' Joanie said, reflexively. She had actually forgotten what she had put on that morning. Her purple skinny jeans, a polka-dot top that Adam had bought her for a birthday present.

'Are you still looking for a job?' Erin asked. 'We need a new member of staff right now.' She paused. 'I can get you a form?'

Joanie hesitated, absent-mindedly turning the pages of her book. She hadn't thought about what she would do next. This place was much better than the Maeyar Visitor Centre. And she had already wasted a lot of money on air travel. The thought made her feel sick. 'Of course,' she said. 'I'd be so grateful for a job here. It seems really nice.' She gave Erin her best smile.

Erin moved to serve another customer and Joanie started filling in the form. It felt so old-school. Her mum had told her to hand out her CV around town, but she knew the world didn't work like that any more. At least, she thought not.

The door opened and she looked up to see Tatey enter the café, his long hair wet from the rain. Oh, God. She hadn't wanted him to come with her. It didn't feel right. He looked too young and out of place.

She stood up, chugged the rest of her tea and plonked her application form by the till, while Erin's back was turned. The other barista was talking to the two girls on the sofa.

'It's really raining outside, so I just thought I'd try and find you . . .' he said, pushing his hand through his unwashed hair.

'Let's get out of here,' Joanie said. She couldn't imagine anything worse than drinking tea with her classmate, this dude in skate pants, pretending to be grown-ups. She could handle the rain.

He looked a little lost. She realized she didn't even know what he was planning to do now that school had finished. That made two of them.

'Have you got the van?' she asked.

'Yeah.' He shrugged, looking at her as he had done in the street. 'I was thinking we could go to the cave.'

10

Cameron, Christmas Eve 2023

Tatey remained quiet and perhaps a little drunk as we walked up Martyr's Street to our old church. There was a familiar sting in the air that felt like Christmas.

'A lot of people there tonight,' I said, digging my bare hands into the pockets of my thin jacket. The cold brought out a latent sense of bravado in me. I felt almost ashamed of wearing a scarf. 'Can't remember the last time I saw Donaldson.' Men like Donaldson didn't wear scarves.

'You two hit it off alright,' replied Tatey, ahead of me, misjudging his step on the cobbled street.

'Yeah, might play some golf with him,' I said. Tatey didn't turn round. He wouldn't be seen dead with a seven iron, even if it were the murder weapon. As casually as I could, I said, 'I didn't know you were friends with Cara.'

'Catch up with her now and again, aye,' Tatey said. I could see only the back of his head, his long hair poking out from under a beanie. I admired his inability to change. We were passing a bare stone fountain in the town square. By spring, it would bloom with geraniums, as it had done every year of my life. No doubt this was still where everyone gathered at New Year, for a reason unknown to me.

I took a deep breath as we turned down a narrow alley. 'Do you ever see Joanie about?'

Still a few steps ahead, Tatey glanced round. Something about his expression made me feel even colder. 'What?' he asked.

'Joanie,' I said. I was sure he had heard me the first time. 'Remember?'

'Alright, I heard ya,' Tatey said, his head down. 'Haven't seen her for a while.'

What did that mean? I let it go for now.

We were passing through the stern architecture of Salvation Street now, a few minutes from St Gregory's. The walls were high and cloistered. Now and then, a gargoyle grinned down at me. Having grown up around here, I took these neo-Gothic arches and medieval windows for granted. Now I was back, they looked more to me like the set of an old horror film. Passing the university chapel, I could still make out the black, smudged outline of what seemed to be a man's face, high in the bell tower. The old story went that the face had appeared sometime in the sixteenth century, after the execution of a martyr, James Black, and never left. His initials were spelled on the cobbled pavement: JB. It was said that students who stepped on them would never graduate.

Candles burned, large and small, on the marble steps to the altar and the stone windowsills. Vanessa had once commented on how much I liked candles for a man, which I denied. She said that if we were ever to get married, that would be the highest cost of the wedding. I hadn't really appreciated the joke. And if I *did* like candles, I hoped that church wasn't the reason why. Even the choir were holding them, as they processed in. I had forgotten about having to do that as a teenager, scared I would set myself alight. It was oddly trusting of the clergy. They had overestimated our maturity. I had forgotten, too, that St Gregory's smelt of stewed berries, a sweet mixture of wine and incense. It was too draughty to take off my coat. I wrapped my scarf even tighter around my neck. People sat with their heads bowed in quiet reflection. That should have been my first indication that this wasn't the Dickensian singalong I had somehow been expecting. It was odd that Tatey had even *wanted* to come here, given what had happened to him. Now, as I stood next to him in the pew, he smelt, unrepentantly, of cigarettes and beer.

The choir began to sing a capella and the hairs rose on the back of my neck.

The angel Gabriel from heaven came,
His wings as drifted snow, his eyes as flame;

We hadn't been brought up in a jolly sort of church. This was not a place of Easter bonnets and harvest festivals. I remembered that now, as I watched the anonymous faces of the choir. This place was old-school and heavyweight. A place that liked ritual and sacrifice and minor keys.

Tatey was whispering the wrong words at me, a glint in his eye. *Most highly flavoured gravy*: the words we had sung at choir practice as young boys, when we had thought no one could hear us.

I looked ahead, trying not to laugh at him while the choir stretched 'Gloria' into seven notes. Tatey had been a good treble back in the day. It was a shame he had hated it. I doubted this choir, who looked much older, passed notes to each other between songs.

Any alcohol that had been buzzing around my system evaporated at the appearance of Father Thomas, who looked even more imposing than I had remembered.

'This isn't Christmas carols,' I whispered, as I knelt next to Tatey, pretending to pray. 'This is Mass.'

'Sorry, dude,' he said, sounding more lucid. 'My bad.'

I glanced over to the door. I was surprised Tatey

had been let in, quite honestly. The time he got kicked out of the choir still made me cringe. One day, when we were in S4 at school, Tatey had stood in the choir stalls, bowed down towards the censer and come back up wearing a Viking helmet. Joanie went into silent, red-faced giggles, while her mother stared furiously from the front row. It turned out Joanie had dared him to do it. I could still picture the thing now, its two holes for eyes. I had found it more awkward and unnerving than funny.

As the Midnight Mass continued, a sense of repentance hung heavier in the air. I didn't care for this. I didn't like feeling guilty and sinful. This was not how I wanted to bring in the Yuletide cheer.

As Father Thomas spoke again, my eyes focused and refocused on the flickering candles, then I noticed a familiar figure in the darkened church. Out of the corner of my eye, I thought I saw Joanie.

Extract from 'Who's Afraid of the Dark?' by Joanie Sinclair, 2012

A loud crash from downstairs woke me up. The only light in my room came from the DVD screensaver, bouncing around like a fly trapped in a jar. It took me a second to remember that I was meant to be home alone. That my family were out of town. It was probably just the cat. I imagined Tinsel jumping and knocking something over downstairs. At that point we had a lot of cardboard boxes stacked in the living room. Then I felt the weight of something on my foot.

Tinsel was sleeping at the end of my bed.

I lay still, waiting, listening for more. I watched the DVD logo silently change colours as it hit each edge of the pink TV.

11

Joanie, June 2013

The exact location of the cave – which could be accessed only at low tide – had been passed down through generations of St Rule teenagers. Joanie and Tatey picked their way over the flat layers of rock, slick with rain. The weather had cleared now. The harbour walls turned into cliffs on their right and the sea roiled on their left. The sea breeze was welcome relief from the stale air of Tatey's van, which had smelt of sweat and takeaways. They had spent about half an hour in there, waiting for the downpour to pass. He had lit a joint, opened the window a crack and talked at length about people from school. The funny thing about Tatey was that he acted so anti-authoritarian, yet seemed to care more than anyone about the minutiae of school politics. He could remember small slights and in-jokes from years ago. He and the deputy head appeared to hate each other with an equal obsession. Couldn't he let it go? It didn't matter any more.

Now, as he and Joanie tried to keep their balance along the wet rocks to the cave, they had lapsed into silence. Grey clouds still brooded over the sea. Tatey's hair hung down over his eyes. He seemed more on edge than usual. He kept fiddling with the end of his hoodie. It couldn't have been the joint: that would barely have touched the sides, given the amount he smoked. It had started to have an effect on her, though. She needed to have her wits about her to avoid the soft, slippery algae that surrounded them. A blast of salty summer wind jolted her senses and a strand of hair wrapped across her face, like a tentacle. She felt a pang of embarrassment. They were too old for this now. It was childish. She was glad they were hidden from view.

A few years ago, when Tatey had first shown Joanie and Cameron the cave, they had pretended to be hiding out while drinking cans of cider and talking about weird shit on the internet. Other times they had planned pranks. Fake, funny phone calls to local businesses. Subscribing their classmates to embarrassing mailing lists, rearranging school property, writing pretend 'letters of complaint' to the local newspaper under an obvious pseudonym, hoping for publication. Once they had even kidnapped Tatey's neighbour's garden gnome and sent a ransom letter for twenty packets of Gummy Bears. Another time Joanie had filmed Tatey walking through the town in a gorilla suit, only to meet another gorilla (Cameron) walking in the opposite direction. Occasionally, they would play tricks on each other. Most of the ideas came from Tatey. He had a particular, largely harmless, sense of humour that became contagious. He had even started posting a few videos online, hoping one would go viral. In the past few months, towards the end of school, Joanie had started to feel she had outgrown these teenage gags. Their video in the library would be the last.

It had been ages since she had been here. Sometimes, when Tatey had messed about in the cave, it had been dangerously daft. One time, he had sprayed aerosol on his arm and said that if he set it alight, his skin wouldn't burn. Of course, he scorched himself while they were stuck up there at high tide. It had been a stupid idea then and this trip to the cave was a stupid idea now. If the tide came in, they would be stranded.

Now, as she saw the opening in the cliffs ahead of her, she had a strange idea that there would be a new group of fifteen-year-olds sitting there instead, or maybe ghosts of themselves from two years ago, doomed for eternity.

Joanie followed Tatey up to the cave's rocky entrance and sat inside on the hard, damp ground. It stank of rotten seaweed. A couple of broken beer bottles lay towards the back. Joanie texted Cara at lightning speed: *Tatey's taken me to the cave.* The message refused to send. She should have remembered there was no signal here.

He wanted to talk to her about history. He said that this was where St Rule had first taken shelter when he landed on the beach from the Mediterranean in the winter of 370 AD.

'I'm sure he'd love to see it now,' said Joanie, feeling strangely sad. 'Why did he even come here?'

'He was shipwrecked.'

'So it was a mistake?' she asked.

He moved closer towards her. 'It's said that sometimes, if you listen carefully, you can hear his boat crashing against the rocks.'

She wanted to gag. His face was close and his arm brushed hers. His hand felt rough against her skin. Then he kissed her, quickly, like it was another dare. His mouth was hot and wet, not at all pleasant. He smelt stale. Something inside Joanie made her want to cry. She didn't want to hurt his feelings but, gently, she pulled away, unable to find the words. He grabbed her wrist. 'We'll just hang here,' he said quietly. 'It's cool.'

It wasn't. She didn't want to stay. The tide outside was coming in steadily, wave after wave below, slowly hemming them in. She missed Adam, the way he touched her. The angle of his jaw, the blue of his eyes. The kiss felt perversely disloyal, like cheating with someone who could have been her brother after all.

'I have to go,' she said. 'I promised my mum.' Promised what, she couldn't say, but pulled herself up instead, and started to clamber back down to the rocks, without a glance back. That would have made her feel even sadder.

Outside the weather had turned obliviously bright.

Her phone buzzed. A reply from Cara: *??? Say more.*

So Joanie's message about Tatey had reached her, but it was no longer funny.

Joanie thrust her phone back into her pocket and made her way over the rocks as fast as she could. Surely he wouldn't follow her. Tourists were gathering near the ruined castle up ahead, at the end of the beach. As she approached, she remembered how its crumbling turrets and walls hid underground passages and a bottleneck dungeon that had terrified her when she was younger.

After almost slipping on some algae, she finally made it to the soft sand of the beach. She looked behind her and saw Tatey climbing down from the cave's mouth. Picking up her pace, she wove past the tour group at the castle's visitor centre and its costumed guides, their medieval cloaks rippling in the summer wind.

She carried on along the cobbles, as fast as she could. Tatey was still some way behind, silent. She realized she was walking up a lane, in the direction of St Gregory's: force of habit. A small part of her wanted to kneel within its cool, dark recesses out of sight to gather her thoughts.

Yet when she passed its gate, memories of singing with Tatey and Cameron in the choir came whirling back to her and she kept walking. On the way up to Salvation Street, she shuddered. The shock of Tatey's ugly kiss in the cave was still reverberating through her. She didn't know what it meant. Had she ever found him attractive? Well, if so, she had been wrong.

Thoughts and images looped in her brain as she hurriedly passed through the town's three main streets, past her school and under the medieval gate to the start of the suburbs. She could have walked the route in her sleep. She didn't know what she wanted. She had an urge to disappear, if just for a while.

'Hang on, you're saying you got a job?' Gary asked on Wednesday, over the blare of the TV.

Joanie looked up from her plate of white fish, peas and potatoes and nodded. Erin had phoned her that afternoon. They liked her, she had said, her voice fuzzy at the other end of the line. They thought she would be a good fit. She had a start date.

Her mother smiled from the armchair in the corner, wedged between two piles of junk, a plate balanced on her knees. She said, in a quiet voice, 'Congratulations, love, that's fantastic.'

Gary, on the sofa, wiped his nose thoughtfully. 'So fast, though. Unusual.'

'Thanks.' Joanie sighed and started to jab the peas with her fork. Erin liked her; it was that simple. She had a job, and if it turned out to be terrible, she'd leave.

Gary broke the silence again. 'Well, don't get me wrong, that's great news. Great news. I'm only saying—'

'She needs to pay the bills, Gaz,' her mother said. Did she?

Joanie dropped her fork on to the plate. 'I've got some stuff to do. Before tomorrow, when I start.' She took her meal upstairs. Trust Gary to try to make her feel small.

Joanie lay on her starry bed, food untouched. She Skyped Cara in the glow of her nightlights. 'I've got a new job,' Joanie said. 'At a student café in town.'

'Oh, really?' Her friend sounded out of breath, having run up the internal staircase of her building to answer the call in time.

'I'm so happy for you.' For some reason, Cara's words sounded flat and disingenuous. Her makeup looked even better than usual.

'Yeah, it's something positive at least,' replied Joanie. 'But tell me about Paris.'

Cara talked briskly about cycling through

Montmartre and drinking cocktails at a new speakeasy. Joanie asked about the Fourchette family, hoping to make Cara laugh, but her friend sounded distracted.

She struggled to imagine Cara's life now. A foreign city where anything could happen. A year to experiment, a year to grow up. Adam had taken that away from her.

Cara, now sitting in her new, plain bedroom, opened her mouth to speak, then stopped.

'No, go ahead. What is it?' Joanie asked. She peered at the room behind her friend, keen to see more of her new home, but the light was terrible.

'You and Tatey,' Cara said flatly. 'You didn't reply to my message. He took you to the cave? Like, what the hell?'

'What?' Joanie sighed. There was an uncomfortable silence. 'Nothing happened. If that's what you mean.'

Cara's voice sharpened. 'It doesn't really sound like nothing.'

'Well, *no*, it wasn't, but . . .' Joanie started, trying to think how to put it. Why had she even agreed to this? She would rather be watching the old pink TV in the corner with Tinsel.

'Come on, we both know you like him,' said Cara. 'You made out like it was a joke.'

'It was a joke. Nothing *happened*.' Joanie heard the whine in her voice. She knew that telling the truth would make everything worse. She doubted Cara would believe her, if she said the kiss had made her body shudder with repulsion.

'You just said something had happened,' Cara replied, raising her eyebrows, her arms crossed.

'No, I didn't.'

'"It wasn't nothing."'

'I didn't say that,' Joanie replied. How could she make her friend change her mind?

'You *basically* did, Joanie. God. Could you not just—'

'What? Go on.'

Cara tilted her head to one side, her orange hair falling over one shoulder.

'It's not like he's your boyfriend . . .' Joanie started quietly, immediately wishing she had kept her mouth shut.

Cara looked over her shoulder, then snapped back at the camera, stony-faced, her red lips pursed. 'I've gotta go.'

'He kissed me and it was gross, OK?' Joanie blurted out.

Cara's screen went black, but not before Joanie had seen her horrified expression.

12

Cameron, Christmas Eve 2023

Joanie's eyes were looking back at me across the dim pews. Her face was older, much older. Her hair was grey and cropped, her face shrunken, like one of my surreal dreams.

'Is that Joanie's *mum?*' I whispered to Tatey, as we shuffled out of the church. He nodded. I had never noticed the similarity. I suppose I had never noticed her much at all until now. A wave of tiredness had hit me and I felt strangely embarrassed by the idea of trying to talk to her. I had some fleeting memory that she was not a friendly person. Intimidating, perhaps, in spite of her small frame.

'Jeezy peeps. The legendary Lynne Byrne,' Tatey muttered back. He turned to his phone. 'Well, this was shite.'

'*Tatey*,' I warned. He needed to keep his voice down.

'My sister's going to drive us home. Says she's in the castle car park already.'

'Wait,' I replied, breaking away from the door queue. 'I just want to say hi.' I had tried to find the humour in coming back to church, but the truth was, guilt flooded my body. I felt it tingling in my arms and legs. I felt it creeping up my spine. I wanted to say sorry to someone, whoever it was. The saints in the stained glass, their eyes rolling back in their heads. The Jesus on the cross, looking down at me with pained disappointment. I had not kept the promises of Confirmation.

I was halfway across the pews to Lynne when Tatey called after me, 'Morris, come on!' jerking his head towards the night outside.

Everyone looked round.

Lynne's hawkish eyes were on Tatey and then me, glaring. I raised my hand and smiled, but her expression didn't change. She seemed not to recognize me, even though I imagined I still looked enough like the fifteen-year-old boy who used to pray here. She turned back pointedly to her conversation with Father Thomas and I followed Tatey out of the church as quickly as I could.

Tatey showed no signs of embarrassment, as the pair of us walked down the narrow, cobbled street towards the castle. I, on the other hand, was mortified. But, then, I hadn't been kicked out of the church as a teenager. Maybe he was trying to prove a point. As for Lynne, perhaps her eyesight wasn't what it used to be.

I studied the ruined castle walls that were perched on the rocks. 'Do you remember when we visited with the Sunday school?' I asked Tatey, pointing to the crumbling stones. A tour guide, dressed as a monk, had told us the place was haunted by a Catholic cardinal whose dead, naked body had been hung from one of the towers.

'I remember that big well thing they had. In the dungeon,' replied Tatey, as we approached Tatey's sister Cassie, leaning against his van in the castle's car park.

'Yeah,' I said, nodding hello to our designated driver. 'The oubliette.'

I remembered how Joanie had screamed down into its vertiginous walls to see how much it echoed.

'No rush,' Cassie said sarcastically to her brother. She looked frozen in her navy trench coat. 'Not like you owe me.' She whacked Tatey's shoulder playfully as we got into his van. I took a back seat by one of the little curtained windows. Tatey passed me yet another can of beer.

'Do you ever *clean* this thing?' Cassie screwed up her nose as she backed out of the car park, past the visitor centre and its poster for the terrifying oubliette.

Now I thought about it, the word 'oubliette' sounded so pretty for something so chilling. From the French word for 'forgetting', it was a deep stone well of a prison, only accessible from the rusty black grate that covered the top. The kind of place in which you were left to rot before being burned at the stake, something else in which St Rule did a good line. It was certainly more than the St Gregory's Sunday-school teacher had bargained for. The feeling of being thrown down there in the dark was not something you forgot easily.

Extract from 'Who's Afraid of the Dark?' by Joanie Sinclair, 2012

After a minute or two, there was another bang downstairs. I clutched the duvet, startled. The crash was followed by movement. Creaking. My house is small and sound carries. I grabbed my remote control and turned off the TV. The room turned black. I didn't want the person downstairs to know that anyone was home. No light came through the thin gap under the door. Slowly and carefully, I got out of bed. Cara? I texted. Are you awake?

13

Joanie, June 2013

So, are you in Vancouver now? A text message from Cameron popped up on Joanie's phone. She had been hoping Cara would text. Irritated, she stopped wiping the café's countertop to reply. It was her first day on the job.

What do YOU think? she began typing, then deleted the words. It was exhausting to explain. An apology would have been nice. In a way, Cameron was partially to blame for this. How could he have seen Adam and Mia go off together into the shadows and not stop them or at least not try to warn her?

She still hadn't heard from Adam.

Joanie shoved the phone back into her pocket, looked at the calm green walls of her new workplace and felt a bit better. It was 7.55 a.m. and she had just watered the plants that twisted around the bookshelves. Morning sun fell on their leaves from the high windows. An earthenware mug of herbal tea sat on the countertop. This wasn't Vancouver, but it was a small step in a new direction. She was wearing a black apron over her favourite daisy-print dress. Adam had said it made her legs look good.

In five minutes, customers would start to trickle in, postgraduates and lecturers grabbing hot drinks for the library next door or taking a seat at one of the small tables. She read through labels on glass tea cylinders, trying to memorize each one: *Cosmic Chamomile*, *Metaphysical Mint*, *Sacred Green*. She was about to take a photograph when Erin's voice stopped her.

'Hi, Joanie. I wanted to introduce you to Mia. You guys will be working shifts together.'

Mia.

The words smashed into her gut, as Joanie slowly turned around.

'Hey.' It was the same Mia. Mia Martinez the life-ruiner, her new colleague, head tilted towards her feet.

Joanie bit her lip and blood rushed to her face. Her hand itched to reach over the counter and yank the girl's ponytail so hard she fell to the floor, with a loud WWE *thump*. She knew she could do it.

'You guys already met?' asked Erin.

Instead of answering, Joanie made a beeline for the bathroom, slammed the door and sat on the closed toilet, pressing the heels of her hands into her eyes. *Fuck you*, she thought, *fuck you, fuck you*. By 'you' she meant Mia, Adam and the world at large. Why couldn't she have this *one* thing? She wanted to text Cara, but Cara was still annoyed with her. She dug her thumbnails into her temples. *One two three four* . . . Erin's voice had sounded so smooth by the side of the road that night. Was it all a sick joke?

After a few minutes, Joanie pulled open the bathroom door and walked straight back out into the sunshine of the Divinity Quad, without a backwards glance, her footsteps reverberating on the flagstones, like an anxious heartbeat. She wanted to carry on through the dark university doors on the other side of the grass and disappear for ever.

'What's going on?' Erin had caught her up outside, her face contorted with concern.

'I can't,' said Joanie. 'She's the girl.'

Erin looked blank.

'She's the girl I told you about. Mia. At the beach. When I met you in the car. She and Adam were . . .' Joanie didn't want to cry again. 'I told you.'

'Oh, *Jesus*,' Erin said. 'I'm sorry.' She reached out and Joanie let herself be hugged. 'Look, Joanie. You can do this. I *really* want you to be on our team. I know you're tough. I like that about you. I'll find a way to make this work. Come back this afternoon.'

She left Joanie standing alone in the manicured garden, staring at roses and fighting violent thoughts.

*

For the next few weeks, Erin tried to keep the peace. She swapped Mia's shift with Vik's, the student who had served her the free drink. While Mia worked, Joanie slept in and watched reality shows on the TV in her bedroom. She had a whole year to kill before she took up her place at Aberdeen to study English. It might as well have been a decade.

Mia was often finishing her shift when Joanie started hers. Instead of feeling anxious, Joanie would try to pretend that Mia was invisible, something drifting out of the building, like an ugly ghost. Joanie made a point of being friendly to Vik while they worked together. She wanted an ally. It didn't hurt that he was good-looking. Mia was a speck of nothing. Less than that.

'Is everything OK?' Vik asked one day when Mia had left.

'Yeah, why?' asked Joanie, trying to play dumb.

'There seems to be an issue between you and Mia,' he replied.

'Really? I don't think so,' she said, flicking her hair over her shoulder.

Vik nodded and got to work, but she caught him looking askance at her now and then.

Despite telling herself she didn't care, Joanie found herself checking Mia's social media at the end of each day, her fingers automatically typing before she could stop them. The girl hadn't posted anything for weeks. The last photo was the day before the beach party. It was simply a picture of a bike and some flowers, overlaid with a heavy filter. Joanie began to hate the bike photo, yet she looked at it again and again. Did Adam like Mia because she was into bikes? Were the flowers significant? It was too much and not enough.

As the days stretched on, Erin would glance at Joanie whenever she checked her apps between serving customers. Cara was having a blast without her, it seemed. Cara's parents had given her an SLR camera before she left and with it she captured the blur of neon streetlights, the sweaty bars, the white symmetry of Paris.

'We're trying to make this a calm space,' Erin said one day, with strained politeness, 'so people can concentrate. I know you're going through a difficult time. I just don't want you to lose focus. Some people find it helpful to keep their phones in the back room. And if you've got anxiety, it's maybe not the best way to deal with it?'

Ouch, thought Joanie. She stopped checking her phone at work, but that left nothing else to stave off boredom except leaf through the battered paperbacks on the shelves. When the café was deadly quiet and Vik had his head in a library book, Joanie read about the life of St Columba and medieval plant remedies. The dream-controlling properties of betony. The use of hyssop against chest phlegm. The teas they sold were not dissimilar. Their Sacred

Green tea was recommended for studying. Their Black Magic tea was recommended for hangovers.

Whenever a customer left behind a newspaper, Joanie would read Adam's horoscope out loud to Vik and imagine unpleasant things happening to him. She wasn't sure Vik appreciated it, but he humoured her. As late June slunk into July, she wondered why Hallowed Ground stayed open over the summer, tucked away from tourists who tramped through the town, hauling their cameras and golf clubs.

She got to know the few regular customers, younger academics who treated the space like an extension of the old library next door.

'Didn't you say the university thought a café would be more profitable than a library?' Joanie asked Vik one particularly quiet day. 'I think they made a mistake.'

'Ha,' he replied, not looking up from some journal article. 'Just you wait until term starts. Everyone loves this place. Not just the Divinity department either.'

She wanted to get to know Vik better, but he was a man of few words. She understood he was a medieval historian from Chennai, who was learning Italian, but that was about it. She wondered who his friends were, if he was going out with anyone.

When she wasn't trying to look clever, reading about monastic life on Iona or remedies for bruising, memories of school occupied Joanie's thoughts. The band night in a draughty village hall where she had first met Adam. She and Cara had gone together, buying cups of value cola from the underage bar, then adding glugs of vodka from a smuggled-in flask. Lots of girls were talking to Adam, but he had taken Joanie's hand and led her out of the hall, as though she had been chosen. They had talked for a little while, then kissed against a mossy wall. Things were never the same after that. Thanks to Adam, everyone forgot about her weird, overstuffed house. Overnight, she was one of the popular kids. She had even introduced Cara to the group.

Usually, when Joanie worked a shift with Erin, it was like her relationship history leaked out of her. She couldn't help it. Somehow the conversation would turn to the fated night she had met Adam, the gut-wrenching betrayal of the beach and everything in between. Joanie even found herself telling Erin about his messy car, his sexist comments, the annoying way he rolled his eyes. She was trying to get rid of it all, but the memories would be waiting for her again the next day.

Erin said very little about herself. She was slightly older than Joanie had thought, studying for a master's in medieval history. She had grown up in California, but didn't mention her family often. The few times Joanie asked after them, Erin's sighs and eye-rolls indicated they weren't in close contact. Her love of nature had grown from hiking trails near her hometown, which sounded remote and hilly, full of sunshine.

Joanie gathered these small nuggets of information over the weeks she shared shifts with Erin, even though they talked endlessly. Their conversations were mainly about Joanie and helping her with her anxiety. Erin seemed to have unlimited time to listen and recommend relaxation and breathing techniques Joanie could try, often walking to the bookshelves as though she knew every title by heart.

Sometimes, Erin would put her hands on Joanie's shoulders and encourage her to take deep breaths in and out, eyes closed, counting. Slowly but surely Joanie began to feel calmer in herself. Cara's pettiness about Tatey wasn't her problem. Good things could come into her life, if she was open to them. Joanie wasn't totally sure if she could call Erin a friend; she was still her manager, but she was big-sisterly and safe.

Like Vik, Erin seemed to have a lot of academic work to do, in addition to her day job: research for her upcoming dissertation. As July slipped into August, David, whom Joanie had learned was a junior lecturer, would arrive most afternoons with files and a notepad to sequester himself in a corner, surrounded by photocopied papers. The café remained quiet, and sometimes Erin would join him at the table. Joanie tried to listen in to their conversations, but it was like trying to decipher a new language.

'Hard at work again?' Joanie asked one day, when David was sitting by himself and Vik was manning the till. David nodded absent-mindedly. She placed his green tea on the small patch of table that wasn't covered with papers, books and Post-it notes. She never saw him pay. Up close, she wasn't sure if he was in his mid-thirties or if his tweed jacket added some years. His glasses looked mismatched to his square-jawed face, a Superman pretending to be Clark Kent.

'Do you know Latin?' he asked, as if snapping out of a daydream. His warm voice had a cut-glass edge that suggested an expensive education.

''Fraid not,' said Joanie.

'Remind me, are you part of the university, Joanie?' he asked, confirming that he actually knew her name. 'I'm so sorry, Erin talks about you all the time, but I've completely forgotten whether—'

'I'm just . . .' What was she? 'I finished school in June.' Two months ago now, and what did she have to show for it? She looked up at Vik, who was reading one of his books.

'I see. Well, I'm giving a talk next door at the beginning of term, if you're interested. It's a week or two away, so I'm trying to drum up support. If you know anyone who would like to come . . .'

He pointed to what she now realised were printed photographs of a yellowed manuscript. 'Pretty groundbreaking stuff actually,' he said, waggling his eyebrows. 'I remember now how much you knew about Maeyar. You'll have to tell me more about your time there.'

No one had ever asked this before. 'Really? I—'

Before Joanie could reply, the door opened and Mia walked in. 'I left my bag,' she said, smiling broadly. Joanie saw Vik look up from the counter.

'Hey-ho!' David called. 'I forgot to give you that book earlier.'

He grabbed a green, clothbound hardback from the table, entitled *Plant and Ritual*.

Joanie felt as though the air had been sucked out of her lungs. She ran past Vik to the toilet and slammed the door, trying desperately to catch her breath.

When she emerged a few minutes later, feeling a little sheepish, she took her station back at the till while Vik served a new customer. Out of the corner of her eye, she saw Erin had come in and was talking to David in a hushed tone.

Erin looked up at her, concerned. 'What's wrong? What happened?' She moved closer, placing her arm around Joanie's shoulders. 'Are you still getting panic attacks?'

Joanie was mortified. It seemed so silly. David was poring over his documents, pretending not to notice. 'Kind of,' she said quietly to Erin as they went to sit together on the other side of the room. 'I've had them for a few years now. It started when . . .' She could feel her chest getting tight and dug her fingernails into the palm of her hand. She pushed the words out. '. . . when someone broke into my house. I was home alone and . . .'

Erin gave her a sympathetic look. 'It's OK,' she said. 'You don't have to say any more. We'll just keep working on it. You and me.' She pulled her close for a hug.

Joanie buried her face in Erin's hair. It smelt of peppermint. 'Thank you,' she breathed. She hated that David had given Mia a book. Of course she was friends with them.

'What is David working on?' Joanie asked Erin, as they wiped down the tables at the end of the day.

'A paper,' Erin replied. 'He's an ethnobiologist. Maybe you could call him a fragmentologist these days. He's translating a medieval manuscript. David was researching Aiden of Maeyar when new fragments of his writing were discovered in the binding of a fifteenth-century text.'

'OK . . .' Joanie wondered why Erin was so excited about papers found in a book, but she pretended to look fascinated.

'He can explain all about it in his talk. It's essentially about transformation. Being an ethnobiologist means he has a crazy knowledge of plants and how people used them in the past, particularly in medieval Europe. That's kind of why we do all the herbal tea here.' Erin bit her lip. 'Listen, I'm worried about you. I know it's not ideal that Mia works here too. I've noticed, from our conversations, that you're a little on edge.'

'What makes you think that?' Joanie asked, pushing in a chair. 'Today was a one off, I . . .'

'Well, you still mention Adam a lot.'

'I'm fine, actually,' Joanie replied, too quickly. She moved to another part of the room. 'Does this place get busier, once the students are back?'

'Oh, yes,' replied Erin. 'And I've been planning some great evening classes. I've been meaning to ask you. During term time, I run a meditation workshop for students here on a Thursday night,' Erin hesitated slightly. 'I've been learning breathing techniques since I was in high school. People like to decompress after sitting in the library all day. It's like lazy yoga. I was thinking it might be helpful to you.'

14

Cameron, Christmas 2023

I came home from midnight mass at two a.m. on Christmas morning to see a figure crouching in the dark hallway of my parents' house. For some reason, the first person I thought of was my neighbour, Stuart Dunn.

As I scrambled to find a light switch, there came the deep whisper. 'Son.' The unmistakable rasp of my father.

'Jesus, Dad,' I murmured back.

'Stay there.'

I could just make out his silver beard in the dim light from the kitchen. A far cry from Santa Claus. It had been so long since I'd seen him. Had he totally lost the plot? 'Why?' I hissed. 'You scared the life out of me.'

'There's a mouse,' he whispered back at me. 'I nearly got it there.'

'Well, *surprise*! I'm home,' I muttered, shaking my head, as I switched on a table lamp and helped him to his feet. My words slurred together a little, thanks to the beers in the back of Tatey's van. I sighed, filled with a sense of happiness and exhaustion. I was home for the holidays and here was my dad, even if he was skulking around in the dark. 'It's great to see you again,' I said.

'You too, son.' Dad put a heavy hand on my shoulder, examining my face with a smile.

I gave him a proper hug, whether he wanted one or not.

'Let's get you a drink,' he said. It was Christmas after all.

'I was just wrapping some presents when I heard the bastard,' my dad explained, pouring me a nightcap in the kitchen. Laphroaig. I perched on the countertop, like I used to when I came home from parties as a teenager, only now my father seemed happy to see me. He had a round, jolly sort of face, but could produce a scowl that would chill you to the bone. A man of few words, he was smiling to himself now, like we were sharing a private joke.

'Daniel Tate still causing mischief these days?' he asked gruffly, sitting down at the kitchen table in front of a plate of mince pies. He looked a little older, wearing a fleece I hadn't seen before. Meanwhile his slippers were the same as ever, practically hanging together at the seams.

'Tatey?' I asked. 'Pretty much, aye, by the sound of it,' I said, trying the whisky.

'Sandwich short of a picnic, that one,' my father replied, with a mouthful of mince pie.

'That's a bit harsh.'

My dad gave me one of his chilly looks that said, *You know I'm right.* 'Won't Vanessa be missing you by now?' he asked, holding out the bottle to top up my glass. 'Your mum willnae like you sitting up there.'

I slid off the counter and, instead of answering his question, sat down beside him and picked at a small blue splatter on the table. My mum would use this surface to paint on when it got too cold in her studio. I had been starting to think of Vanessa much less often. There had even been one or two clear days when I didn't think of her at all. London felt far away, physically as well as mentally. At some point, I should let my parents down gently. I would start by mentioning that things weren't quite right between Vanessa and me, that we'd been having doubts about getting married. It was a sanitized version of what had really happened. I would leave out the cold silences and crying. Yet I was still looking at the blue paint without having said a word.

In my peripheral vision, my father gave a single nod. You didn't always have to explain. Just then, something small pinballed from the kitchen, along the hallway, bumping against the skirting board.

'That damn mouse . . .' my dad grumbled, his eyes fierce beneath his bushy brows.

I thrust out my hand to stop him getting up and

dropped my voice to a whisper, mindful of my mother. 'It's nearly three a.m. Probably time we turned in, eh?'

'Oh, aye,' he replied, running a hand over his beard. 'Sleep changes when you retire. But you're right. Your mother wants us to go and see Kirstin the morra.'

'Dad . . .' I paused, thinking of our neighbour Stuart skulking about the garden. 'Is everything OK with you and Mum?' My throat felt dry.

'Of course it is!' he said brusquely. Something flickered across his face as he took a closer look at me. 'How?'

'Just checking,' I said, thinking of my mother's strange reaction when I had arrived at the house this morning. Meeting Tatey at the station seemed like a week ago.

'Uh-huh,' he said. 'My grandfather would have said, *Ye've got mair in your heid than the spane puts in*, Cam.'

Whenever he said this, it wasn't a compliment.

Upstairs, I crashed on to my freshly made bed, whisky still warming my throat. I pulled the duvet up to my ears and tried to drift off. While my body ached, thoughts raced around my brain like hungry mice. Maybe my dad was right. There was way more in my head than a spoon could ever put in. I had a tendency to over-think things. After a while, I texted my ex-fiancée. *Merry Christmas, Vanessa.*

Extract from 'Who's Afraid of the Dark?' by Joanie Sinclair, 2012

I opened the door as quietly as I could, but it still made a loud creak. I stood stock still, my bare feet on the carpet. Downstairs was silent. I edged over to the banister and peered down into the stairwell. I thought I heard another bump. Too big for a mouse, or any such creature. Whoever was stumbling downstairs was stumbling in darkness. My family would have put some lights on. Then the noise became louder. Someone was walking towards the stairs. I felt around for my phone and started calling Mum. It rang off. Hello, this is Lynne Byrne's phone. Please leave a message after the tone. *I listened closely in the dark. A man was down there, I was sure of it. A chill rushed through my body. I wondered if this was the way I would die.*

15

Joanie, September 2013

It was seven p.m. on the Thursday after Fresher's Week and the lights of Hallowed Ground were off. Blinds had been rolled down over the windows, blocking out the waning summer light. Vik appeared silently and helped Joanie and Erin to move the tables and chairs to one side. He didn't say much, as usual, but she kept finding herself looking at him. When he smiled back, she felt flustered. He didn't seem to notice, just rolled out his mat while another student arrived, then two more. Erin left the door open for a while longer, eventually realizing that no one else was coming.

As she lay on the floor, Joanie eyed the heaped outline of the furniture merging with the bookshelves. She didn't like a room to be too dark: it made her panicky. She could feel her breath start to stall in her chest. Like Erin had said, she needed to overcome her fears. The three large candles helped, burning in different corners of the room.

When Erin moved from body to body, laying a coarse blanket over each, it felt comforting, as though she were tucking them up in bed. For the first time in weeks, Joanie felt a small sense of joy.

A soft drone started to flow from the speakers, like friendly insects. All other thoughts drifted away. Erin spoke calmly as she walked around the room. 'Quieten your eyes. Don't fully close them. Let them drift in and out of focus. If any thoughts of the day enter your head, push them to one side.'

Mia. Joanie thought. *Adam.* Then she let the sound flush them out.

'You can see waves, washing in and out on the shore,' Erin continued. 'Our beautiful rocky coastline that you see every day.'

The cave. It was there and then it was gone. Joanie bit her lip. *The break-in.* She let out a deep breath. Acres of empty sand filled her imagination.

'The sun is warm and bright,' Erin said. 'You can see blue butterflies in the sand dunes. The air is still. If you listen carefully, you may start to hear the waves.'

The instrumental sound merged with a soft rush of saltwater, pushing forward and then withdrawing across smooth pebbles. 'Listen carefully.' Erin started to name different body parts sequentially, asking the attendees to relax. Joanie imagined she was lying on a warm beach as she listened to the pulse and rush in the darkened room. There was just this, nothing before and nothing after. Relief unfurled inside her like a flower.

The next evening, Joanie lay on her bedroom floor, illuminated by her night lights, and closed her eyes. Her phone played meditative music, the closest she could find to Erin's playlist. She tried to get the feeling back. She imagined the empty beach again and the slow waves, but it didn't look the same.

The door jerked open. 'What are you doing?' her mother hissed. 'You'll wake Elise.'

Joanie glared at her and picked herself up, embarrassed. She spent the rest of the evening staring out of her window at the street. She could see Graham's house from here. She imagined his family enjoying a Friday takeaway and an action movie. She had been over there a few times when she was younger, but not any more. Her mother never had anyone over because it was 'too much of a mess', which was an understatement. Once a girl at school had joked about never seeing the inside of her house. 'What are you hiding in there?' she had asked.

'Just a couple of nukes,' Joanie had replied, in a way that had made everyone laugh. When she was thirteen, she had told her classmates that a poltergeist was terrorizing her home, messing everything up. She had wished it were true.

The best thing about the meditation class was that Mia hadn't come to it. Every time Joanie passed

Mia in the café, she wanted to grab her phone off her and read her text messages, searching for Adam. Except, of course, she never used it.

When Joanie was back at work, she asked Erin as much as possible about meditation and sound baths.

'Thursday was so good,' Joanie said. 'I'm going to be there every week.'

Erin reached into her bag and pulled out a book titled *Breath and the Mind*. 'This is how David and I hit it off,' she said, holding it out to Joanie. 'We were both interested in transcendental experiences.'

'I thought he was into Latin,' Joanie said, 'and not having a phone.'

Erin laughed, shaking her head. 'He studies rituals, like I said. Did you decide to come to his talk? I think you'd find it really interesting.'

'I'm there,' Joanie replied, taking the book. She wanted to know everything.

16

Cameron, Christmas Day 2023

I dreamed I was in the oubliette. The forgetful place. It was pitch black and I was looking up at a tiny circular grate, far above my head. Then I touched the walls and realized they were the metal shelves of Hallow's Hill school library. I was standing in an aisle so narrow that my shoulders brushed against book spines. I could feel something or someone watching me. The aisles were like a dark maze. I thought I heard a mouse. I looked through a gap in the books to my right and saw Joanie's legs lying on the floor.

Then something else flickered in my peripheral vision. It was a rabbit, bounding along the aisle to my left. I took one turn and then another, but couldn't find a way to reach either of them. Up ahead, in the dark, I saw a figure in a Viking helmet. When I woke up my mouth was dry and I remembered it was Christmas Day.

My sister Kirstin and her family still had norovirus,

so for the first time since I could remember, it was just my parents and me. I had borrowed a spare, scratchy dressing-gown that stopped at my knees. My parents sat at the breakfast table, drinking cups of tea. My mother without her glasses and my father with his unbrushed hair looked a little bewildered. They kept scrolling through their phones to show me photos of my nephew Finn. Unbelievably, he was almost four now and seemed to have grown in every photo. His hair was the same colour as mine.

'Why don't I make us waffles?' I asked, thinking of the contraption I had spotted in the cupboard.

'If you've got any bacon, I wouldn't say no,' my dad replied, wiping some toast crumbs from his mouth.

My mum tutted, in her well-practised way. 'You know I've got bacon. Smoked salmon. Blinis. Let Cammy make what he wants.'

'Of course,' I said. 'Bacon to go with them.' I wanted to show my gratitude. It wouldn't be long before my mum got to work on a joint of beef and my dad would start making his beloved roast potatoes. Under the tree, I could see the presents my mother had rushed out to buy me yesterday. It had been very sweet of her, even though my dad had rolled his eyes. Whisking eggs in my wee dressing-gown, I felt an unfamiliar sense of happiness.

'Mum, this is far too much for the three of us, my God,' I said, grinning, when I saw the size of the roast. We were sitting at the table, right by the garden window. Things looked bleak out there.

'Well, Cammy, it's not all for us. I did say we'd nip down to Edinburgh and drop some off with Kirstin.'

'Won't it get cold?' I asked, only half joking. A roast wasn't a great idea when it came to gastroenteritis.

'Come on, greedy guts, let's get started,' said my dad, holding one end of a cracker out to me. 'Otherwise it'll get cold for us all.'

After we had read out the terrible cracker jokes, we ate in relative silence, our cutlery scraping against the best china. I had missed my family's Christmas dinner. Vanessa's family would have mustard dumplings and red cabbage alongside roasted goose legs. Possibly the reason I had been there two years in a row. My parents hadn't seemed to mind. Rather they sounded pleased we were getting on so well. My mother had been over the moon about the engagement, so I had no idea how to break the news to her.

Now was not the time, anyway. There was something special about this, as quiet as it was. As I helped myself to seconds, I started to wonder if there really would be enough for the others. As the meal went on, my parents became a little preoccupied, my father muttering about traffic on the Queensferry Crossing. I wished he would enjoy the moment instead of rushing through his roasted veg. I looked out at the garden and noticed small flakes of snow had started to fall.

By the time we had finished the main meal and begun to open presents, I could tell my dad was champing at the bit. He tore open the Raymond Chandler omnibus I had bought him, while my mum gave me a hug for her art-workshop voucher. 'That's so thoughtful, Cammy.'

They – or rather she – had bought me Fair Isle socks and a large, leather-bound notebook, as my bonus coming-home present. Maybe my taste was finally catching up with theirs, but I loved them.

'Are you sure you don't want to come to Edinburgh with us?' she asked. Perhaps it was selfish of me, but I couldn't really see the point of the car trip. I didn't know why we couldn't just postpone the family gathering until Kirstin, Paul and Finn were feeling better. Everyone was going to be OK.

'I'm not feeling great,' I said. It wasn't exactly true, but the previous day had exhausted me. 'I think I'll give pudding a miss, if that's OK.' A small sacrifice I could make up for later.

Once they had left, laden with presents, I lay on the sofa in front of *Home Alone*, managing to eat Christmas cake and scroll social media at the same time. Unlike some of my other friends, who were all sitting around tables heaving with food, Mia had posted a photo of the windblown South Sands. *Spending this year with my flatmate*, the caption read. I went on her profile page again. Book reviews and wild swimming. Once a nerd, always a nerd. At the pub the night before she had sounded worried that Joanie wasn't there. I wanted to message her to ask her what she'd meant, but I'd make myself wait until after Christmas.

I heard the sound of something being pushed through the letterbox. A Christmas card from a neighbour. Perhaps Stuart Dunn, who seemed fond of stoating about the place in his fishing gilet.

The envelope was addressed to me in block capitals. Inside was a small Christmas card, with a wintry scene on the front. Written in a scrawl, it read: *Dear Cameron. Kindly leave things be. This is a warning. Stop asking about Joanie.*

I dropped the card on to the table, as though it were scalding hot. What on earth? The only person I had really spoken to at any length was Tatey. Maybe one or two people at the pub. It didn't make sense.

I went upstairs and felt the urge to rip up the card and flush it down the toilet, but then shoved it in my wardrobe, just in case I needed some sort of evidence. My parents were too old to worry about something like this. I tried to lie down and zone out to a podcast, but I couldn't relax. The bedroom no longer felt like mine. My throat felt dry. *Leave things be.*

I moved the shells to one side and climbed on to the deep windowsill again. The light was fading and the village was deadly quiet. All the evidence that

I had once slept in this room had been relegated to two plastic boxes on top of the wardrobe. I lay there, trying to remember what was inside.

Then I had a brainwave. I hefted down one of the boxes and opened it to find my old yearbook. The inside cover was filled with messages from my former friends.

I studied Tatey's: *And if you gaze long enough into the abyss the abyss will gaze back at you.* The man was a walking book of Nietzsche quotes. It was carefully written, spidery perhaps, but a different shape from that of the message I now held in my hand.

I studied the scene on the front of the Christmas card. It was pretty average, like the kind you buy in a multipack at a charity shop: a rabbit in a snowy field set against a night sky, a cosy cottage in the background. That wasn't much to go on.

I turned back to the yearbook messages and doodles, scanning through to see if any caught my eye.

Take care and good luck at uni: Graham Donaldson's perfunctory note, written in bunched-up lettering. It was so impersonal, you would almost think we weren't friends. It didn't look like a match, but it made me remember we had agreed to meet up.

As I ran my finger over the page, Joanie's cute, bubbly handwriting caught my eye. *Take care, Cameron, it's been great knowing you x*. All these messages were written as if we were never going to see one another again. About a decade had passed and Joanie seemed to be the only person for whom that was the case.

When none of the messages stood out to me, I leafed through the pages inside. Photos from the trip to the local Isle of Maeyar, a year or so before Joanie started working there. We had learned about the Danish raids and waved kitsch plastic swords on the short ferry trip home.

My class was standing in a group by the cliffs, wearing Viking helmets. I spotted a scrawny Tatey in his. A few weeks later he would use it to play the prank at church. All the parents had thought Tatey had gone off the rails. It didn't take much to shock them. St Gregory's had informed the school, who had kept an eye on him for any further suspicious activity. From then on, Tatey spent every Sunday morning blissfully alone watching TV.

Then I flicked through the yearbook photos. Pages of startlingly young seventeen-year-olds. Looking through now, boys I had once admired seemed childlike and vulnerable. I taught children of the same age and yet I remembered my friends so differently. Mia's photo was barely recognizable. She wore a serious expression behind those unfashionable glasses. I remembered how pretty she looked at the pub. Adam had obviously seen that, when we were back at school.

His own photo jumped out at me. Somehow, he still managed to look photogenic under the cheap school lighting. I had always found something slightly strange about him under his coolly confident exterior. Something insecure and controlling. I remember Joanie wearing a dress he had bought her. It had been odd to witness her transformation from the slightly goofy tomboy in church to a girl who wore high heels and lipstick. A girl whom everyone, myself included, saw as cool.

And here was my own photo: pudgy and bewildered in a blazer. It struck me now that London had eroded that boy, with its air pollution and sweaty tube carriages and seven-pound pints, the late-night essay marking and the disappointing dating apps. I shook my head. I wished I could have warned him.

I turned a page and Joanie stared back at me in a shirt and tie. Her smile was like a gut punch. She had been planning a gap year in Canada, I remembered. Then at Boar's Raik she had run off into the pitch black, a band of flowers slipping out of her long hair.

It's a little concerning, Mia had said, yesterday evening, about Joanie. Now this card. Maybe someone had overheard us talking. I could still remember seeing Mia and Adam walking off into the sand dunes together, but I had been too focused on Chloë and trying to look cool. I should have done something.

BLUFF

I searched the internet on a whim. *June 2013. Joanie Sinclair. Hallow's Hill School.* Even if she had married, changed her name, something should have come up. Someone I knew had to be connected to her still, surely. And yet I could find nothing.

Extract from 'Who's Afraid of the Dark?' by Joanie Sinclair, 2012

There was no question about it, we had a burglar. As quickly and silently as I could, I crawled back under my duvet and lay there. I thought of Cara. Was she awake too, throwing up sushi? I texted her and prayed for a reply.

Later, I would wonder why I didn't hide in the wardrobe, like they do in movies. If I had tried, I might have found the small space too stuffed with clothes. Anyway, I didn't think of it. I wasn't a sneaky fifteen-year-old girl. I was good.

17

Joanie, September 2013

It was two weeks into the start of term, and Joanie walked out into the Divinity Quad to join the small crowd who had gathered for David's talk. Several students looked like teenagers, and she realized that, in another life, this could have been her, talking earnestly with her peers about a Dr Henderson. David. She could hear a charge of excitement in their low voices. Yet when she listened closer to two girls next to her, the conversation was far from academic.

'I think he's trying to grow a beard,' the girl standing in front of her said.

'*No*, he must have just forgotten to shave,' her friend replied. 'I want to ask him where he gets his glasses from, though. They're just so . . .'

'*Scholarly.*'

They started to giggle.

When Erin opened the door, they all filtered past the front desk to a seating area, facing aisles stacked with books. This was the first time Joanie had set foot in the library. The high, arched ceilings were the same shape as those in Hallowed Ground next door, but painted baby blue and white. There were glass cabinets on either side, displaying antiquated tomes that reminded Joanie of spell books. She could see why students preferred this place to the brutalist architecture of the main library, which could have been mistaken for a car park.

A lot more people were here than there had been for the meditation class, that was for sure. Some were hipsters, in skinny jeans or tea dresses. Others were new agey, in tie-dye and Jesus sandals, the same people who did circus stunts at the beach. It was an odd combination.

Joanie spotted Erin in the front row of library chairs, facing a lectern. She had saved her a seat. It felt strange sitting in this place. She was in her hometown, surrounded by people who looked only a little bit older than her, but she recognized no one. It was as though she had found an escape portal to a parallel town. The people talked quietly as if they knew each other, or stared straight ahead, waiting.

When David walked up to the lectern there was a loud round of applause. He gave a little nod and arranged some documents, while a student pushed a large, metal device towards him.

'Thank you, everyone, for joining me this evening.' David beamed. 'Thank you to Hallowed Ground for hosting us and to Mia for helping me record this session for anyone who is unable to make it.'

Joanie spotted Mia standing at one side of the room. Of course. What a wee sook.

'If I could ask everyone to kindly switch off their phones, those of you who have them.'

A soft murmur of laughter rose from the audience.

'Thanks to my friends and esteemed colleagues for joining me today. This is somewhat out of character for me, but I wanted to share some of my research with you rather urgently. I will explain as we go, but I am recruiting volunteers for this project. If you're interested, come and see me after the talk.'

Joanie could hear students shift in their seats and whisper behind her. She clearly wasn't the only one who was intrigued by the idea.

The lights dimmed and the device projected light on to a blank, white wall. 'I prefer this to PowerPoint,' he said. He had a way of speaking that could make just about anything sound interesting. He slid a plastic sheet on to the projector and a fuzzy image of a white figurine appeared on the wall. It was a little man in a pointed hat, holding a sword. He had cartoonish eyes and a big row of teeth.

'A piece from the Lewis Chessmen. It was carved from walrus tusk, somewhere between 1150 and 1200 CE. Can you see he's biting his shield there? This marks him out as a berserker. What caused him to bite his shield? It was an animalistic rage state. A rage that made him superhuman and murderous.

It is suggested that the berserker, who would wear the skin of a bear or a wolf, became the basis for the myth of the werewolf. He was half man and half animal.'

Joanie had stopped picking the bobbles off her jumper. The description sent a chill through her body. She remembered the night her house had been broken into, when she was home alone. She had heard the footsteps downstairs, then crashing, like anger reverberating. She remembered feeling trapped in her bed, unable to move, completely terrified.

Another slide appeared on the projector: HENBANE.

'One theory,' David was saying, 'is that this violent rage or *Berserkergang* was chemically induced by a plant or a mushroom. Now, there was one person who witnessed this rage first hand and wrote about it. His name was Aiden and he lived through the Danish raid on the Isle of Maeyar in 876. As many of you know, this is my field of research. This is my guy. His account of the raid is by far the most visceral we have to date. It's extraordinary.

'What's even more extraordinary is that, having witnessed this massacre, he went about trying to discover what brought on the berserker state in these men. I'm interested in his theories.'

He pointed at the word projected on the wall. 'For those unfamiliar, henbane is part of the same family as potatoes, tomatoes and aubergines. Also, deadly nightshade. In fact all of those plants are nightshades in different forms. Some of them you eat in a salad, others would kill you. Henbane is perhaps our most unexplored. Aiden of Maeyar was someone who tried to research its properties.

'In general, this plant, otherwise known as *Hyoscyamus niger*, is incredibly important to medieval history and yet we still know so little about it. It is a common European weed that is widely believed to have played a central part in witch hunts. The long, rambling testimonies of these men and women could well have been caused by a plant that makes you hallucinate. It is common for someone on henbane to believe they are flying through the air.

'But could this be applied to the berserkers?

'Earlier this year there was an incredible discovery of medieval manuscript fragments, in St Rule's special collections library, binding a volume from the fourteenth century about herbal medicine. These fragments turned out to have been written by none other than Aiden of Maeyar himself, on the properties of *Hyoscyamus niger* – henbane – and its usage. I have been carefully translating these fragments from the original Latin. To give you a sense of their significance, I would love to read you a short extract now, documenting the first time that Aiden tried the plant himself.' He raised his voice as he read his translation. 'A terrible ice flooded my veins and my teeth rattled. Finally, my blood boiled in my body and a wild fury – *animositas fera* – came over me. My soul – *animus* – took on the strength of a wolf that night.'

As David talked at length about the translation process, Joanie glanced around the room. Members of the audience were writing feverishly in notebooks or listening with wide-eyed concentration. Surely this wasn't what every university lecture would be like, Joanie thought.

'To conclude,' David said, causing Joanie to snap back into the room, 'so little has been written about the Danish invaders and their use of henbane that this finding has the potential to blow open our understanding of their practices. I believe that it could be a vastly misunderstood plant, with potential to have beneficial properties.'

As people mingled after the talk, a number of students formed a semi-circle around David, keen to hear more. Joanie drank a free cup of herbal tea, provided by Hallowed Ground, as she tried to listen from a distance. Erin was standing next to David, hanging on to his arm. When Joanie gave up trying to follow the conversation, she moved on to warm Chardonnay, served by a guy with acne. She peered at antiquated books in cabinets. An old map and a display of religious texts. Eventually, feeling unsteady on her feet, she made her way out of the library, still holding the plastic wine glass.

Mia was slouching in the doorway, smoking a cigarette by herself. She tried to look away, but Joanie caught her eye.

'I don't even know what to say to you.' Joanie peered into her drink. She wanted to throw the dregs into her classmate's face.

Mia flushed. 'I've been wanting to talk to you,' she said. Her throat was croaky.

Joanie could barely hear her. 'What would he even see in you?' She deployed her meanest tone, the one she usually used for talking back to her mother.

'Adam lied to me. He said he'd broken up with you. We'd been seeing each other a while.' Mia sounded pathetic.

'I don't like the fact you're here. Let's put it that way.'

Mia didn't seem to have an answer. She just shrugged and nodded. 'I don't talk to him any more, if that helps.'

'Piss off,' said Joanie. She finished her glass as she started to walk home in the dark. It was nearing eleven thirty, far later than she had agreed to be home.

18

Cameron, Boxing Day 2023

'Yeah, I remember Joanie. How?' Graham Donaldson asked, while watching me line up a shot. He had a face that would go far in the World Poker Championships.

I hesitated and looked up from the small white ball in front of me. 'I'd like to see how she's doing these days,' I said. It was Boxing Day morning and we were out on a links course called the St Nicholas, one of the more affordable places to play. Perhaps he was trying to put me off my game.

In reply, Donaldson merely gave me the faintest of nods, impatient for me to get going so we could finish the hole. The sea wind made my eyes water as I tried to focus. I swung with a grimace and the ball pitched neatly on to the green.

'Always got something up your sleeve, Morris,' said Donaldson, in his signature monotone. 'Always hiding something in your back pocket.'

'Am I fuck,' I said, laughing. It was a fluke that I

was somehow doing better than he was. That was the nature of golf. He had yanked his cap backwards in frustration. I was surprised, after all this time, that I still remembered how to hold a club. The words of our PE teacher, Mr Piper, came back to me: 'I want to see you standing like gorillas!' he would bellow, walking up and down the line of freezing teenagers, karate-chopping any rigid knees and elbows.

Most importantly, this game was the only way Donaldson would talk to me. Really talk.

'Her family still lives on my road, you know. Cannae mind the last time I seen her,' he said. 'Cannae say I've *looked* for her, mind you.'

'Oh yeah?' I asked.

There was a pause while he putted his ball at the hole and missed. *Nae joy*, I thought, tapping mine in. I was winning. He congratulated me by raising his eyebrows, then continued our conversation, like it was nothing.

'Definitely havenae seen anyone from that family while I've been back. I remember she was always getting on the bus for Maeyar. That must have been at school. Time flies, eh?'

Maybe something he'd say would help me to understand the card. I tried to act casual, but I was soaking up all of this information like a flannel. 'I remember seeing her at the end of school. The party down at Boar's Raik,' I said. 'I can't believe it was ten years ago. A whole decade. It's strange, don't you think? Nobody knows where she is. I want to know what happened. It's almost like she disappeared.'

Donaldson looked at me out of the corner of his eye as he wiped his golf ball with his towel. 'She was about. I definitely seen her.'

'You messaged her? Recently?' I asked. This would change everything.

'No, no. The night of that party. She'd been excited about that bloody trip with Thingme. Then he shagged that bird or whatever it was.'

'Right,' I said. 'The people we had a drink with two nights ago, you mean.'

'Did you not message her at the time? Check she was OK?' he asked.

'No, I . . .' Had I? 'Maybe I did and she just didn't reply.'

'Right,' said Donaldson, drawing the conversation to a close. We'd walked to the next hole. He tee'd off. The sound of a driver cleanly hitting a golf ball is still intensely calming to me, like the chime of Tibetan finger cymbals.

'So, she was OK?' I asked, walking up to the tee. Donaldson knew not to answer yet. There was something equally soothing in the ritual of setting up a shot. The way one hand slid into the other's grip. The flex of the arms, the bend of the knees, feet firm, chin up. I let out a deep breath. It was about connecting. Being both strong and relaxed as you twisted into the same shapes again and again, along the miles of windblown space. I played the best shots when my mind was in an engaged, yet pleasantly empty state.

A whip of air. A walnut crack.

I had hit a belter down the fairway, a few yards past Donaldson's ball.

He let out a grave whistle. 'Someone's been down the range.'

I tried not to look too pleased with myself.

'To answer your question,' he continued, as we hefted our bags on to our backs, 'she was fine. I'm sure she was. I sometimes messaged if we were at the same party, just to check if she was going home or had already left, you know. Sometimes Cara would give us a lift.'

'Oh, yeah? How did you get home that time?' We began to walk together, golf clubs clacking.

'What – from that end-of-school party?'

'Aye.'

'Not a scooby, man. Funny. You can always mind *being* at a party, but never how you got home, eh?' This was Graham's idea of a joke, though his face stayed dead straight and his mouth barely moved as he spoke. 'I cannae mind the rest of that night, or any of them, really. Wonder why, eh?' He sucked his teeth. 'All I know is she was fine. I text her. I'm positive. Nothing to worry about.'

'And did you see her after that?'

He stood in silence for a few moments. 'No. I don't think so, now you mention it. Maybe I went on holiday, or uni. I don't really know. I used to like her photos online. She was always posting what she was doing. Then that stopped, aye. The family keeps to themselves. That I do know.' He was looking ahead at the green. 'Want to make this game a bit more interesting?' he asked, looking me in the eye. 'I've been going easy on you, just to give you a fair chance.'

'Why not?' I said, trying to remember how much cash was in my wallet. I knew the subject of Joanie was closed. At least for now.

Extract from 'Who's Afraid of the Dark?' by Joanie Sinclair, 2012

As I heard the intruder climb the stairs, my heart became my entire body. There was no before, there was no after. Boom. Boom. Boom. Heartbeat. Footsteps. That's the only way I can describe it.

19

Joanie, September 2013

When Joanie stumbled into the darkened living room, she thought she was alone. A long time ago, the light switch had been blocked off by a tower of cardboard boxes. Then, as time passed, the cardboard boxes had been buried under a layer of what Joanie called 'ephemera'. Ephemera sounded like the name of a pretty Victorian governess, a character from one of the books she had read as a child. Ephemera was all over the house, on every spare inch of carpet. Ephemera covered the bags of baby clothes and unopened boxes of nappies and broken gadgets and gizmos that her mother claimed she was going to fix. There were towers of fast fashion and turrets of charity-shop knick-knacks. Standing among it, in the dark, made Joanie short of breath. She wanted to reach for the light of her phone, but it was dead. Somewhere among all this junk, to the right of the leatherette armchair, was a battery-powered light—

There was a cough, short and raspy.

Joanie clanked into something metal that clattered to the floor.

'Have you been drinking?' her mother croaked, from the direction of the armchair. At the click of a switch, her face illuminated: half harsh light, half grotesque shadow. Mother and daughter faced each other, gargoyle versions of themselves, amid the ragged edges of the ephemera.

'Not even a hello?' Joanie said, masking her fright with sarcasm. 'No, I just tripped over. You could have left the light on.'

'You woke me up,' her mother said. 'I was sleeping here.'

Of course. Her half of the bed was probably piled with stuff now too.

'I can see you smirking,' her mother went on. 'If you wanted a hello, you could have told me where on earth you were. Anyone would think you don't live here any more. Look at you. I don't know what you've been doing, but you're a mess.'

Joanie laughed then, a bitter exhalation. '*I'm* a mess?' She looked around. She'd lost track of time, but surely it wasn't that late. 'I wonder where I got that from.'

'You get it from your father,' her mother replied. She was being openly hostile now. The gloves were off. 'No wonder things aren't working out for you.'

Her mother couldn't have been talking about

Adam. But she was. Joanie staggered back, as if she had taken a physical blow. Her heel hit the sharp lid of a plastic storage box.

'At least I'm not a hoarder,' she spat back, making for the stairs before she could see her mother's face.

In her bedroom, she hit the switches of each of her nightlights, the argument still reverberating in her ears. Nobody brought up her dad. This was a new low. She wanted to phone him then and there, probably interrupting a make-out session with a girlfriend who was barely older than she was. That was unfair. She steadied her breath. He cared about her. *Not enough for you to live with him*, a voice in her head said. *That* was unfair. It just hadn't worked out, partly because her mother had been so interfering. Her mother who *barely saw her any more?* Isn't that what she had wanted? Joanie was simply a reminder of her previous life, along with all the other shit that hung around the house. She was the product of a holiday fling with a married man that had resulted in her mother's religious conversion. Her come-to-Jesus moment.

Joanie picked up her phone to text Cara, then remembered that Cara thought she had stolen Tatey. How ridiculous. Anyway, her phone's battery had died. No matter.

Joanie lay in the lamplight, breathing to a meditation track on her laptop. Waves rolled in and out of some other shore, beckoning her.

20

Cameron, Boxing Day 2023

'Joanie, aye, she used to work at the uni,' Donaldson's older sister Sarah said to me, as we sat in front of the football, eating sandwiches his mother had made from their leftover Christmas dinner. Things had taken a turn on the golf course: I had ended up losing to Donaldson. My pockets were significantly lighter, so I was enjoying as much free food and drink as possible. They were the kind of family who ate exactly the same festive meal every year: turkey with cranberry sauce and chestnut stuffing. Sarah had told me so. My family weren't so different, but part of what I liked about Graham and his were their reliability. They were also a family of golf fanatics. On the walls of their living room hung posters from the 1930s, depicting art-deco figures swinging clubs in plus-fours or cloche hats. ST RULE BY RAIL, one said, with a steam train puffing across the coastline in the background.

While Graham was monosyllabic, Sarah could talk enough for two people. 'I don't remember what Joanie did,' she was telling me now, with her bright, freckly face, 'but I remember I saw her around town when I worked at Altman's. Wasn't she with that Adam guy?'

'No,' I said, trying not to sound like a teacher. 'They broke up at the start of that summer.'

'Maybe it was Tatey,' Graham said. I thought he hadn't been listening.

'Hmm, it was such a long time ago,' Sarah said. She bit her thumbnail absently. 'I thought I saw her with one of those guys in your year, when I was working that summer.'

'She's got a great memory.' Their mum, Siobhan, entered the living room with a plate of pigs in blankets. 'I've always said that, haven't I?'

'Do you even know what we're talking about?' Sarah said. She turned to me. 'I'm hardly here. I stay in Dundee now. Mum, do you remember Lynne's daughter, Joanie? Have you seen her recently?'

Her mother made a face, as she sat down in the armchair opposite me. 'Och, they keep themselves to themselves, don't they? Getting any chat out of Lynne's like trying to get blood out a stone. No, I'm being unfair. Did her daughter go abroad or something? I'll ask, next time I see her. But you know what she's like. Barely comes oot the hoose. Miss Havisham.' I could tell from the twinkle in her eyes that she was loving this unexpected chance to gossip.

'Maybe I'll drop by on my way back,' I said, as if this wasn't the entire reason I had invited myself over to Graham's after our game of golf. I had been trying to summon the courage to do it, the whole time we had been eating lunch. My hand went to take the small Christmas card out of my pocket to show it to them, but I thought better of it. *This is a warning.* It was a horrible thing that would set people talking. I wasn't sure that was what I wanted, at least not right now. Tatey or Adam: Sarah had seen her with one of them.

'Right,' I said, with a decisive knee slap. 'That's me away. If I don't see you through the week . . .'

'I'll see you through a window,' Graham replied emotionlessly, his eyes fixed on the post-match analysis.

'Sounds creepy when you say it.' His mother laughed. I pictured him looking out across the road at night, noticing when Joanie's light was on and when it wasn't.

When I walked into the cul-de-sac, a rush of memory hit me harder than I had thought possible. The nubby branches of the cherry tree in her front garden and breeze blocks shaped like flowers. The brown pebble-dashed walls, the crazy-paving path. As I stood on the doorstep, my reflection was distorted in a textured-glass panel. The doorbell still played the same cheery tune. I must have been to her home only a handful of times, but it was not somewhere you forgot.

I had, however, completely forgotten about Gary, her stony-faced stepfather, until he answered the door. I must only have seen him standing in the front row at church.

'Hi,' I stuttered. 'Graham mentioned—' For a split second I saw Joanie running up the stairs in the darkened hallway. Long hair, pale limbs. Unmistakably a young, teenage girl.

'Mentioned what?' the man barked. He had puffy cheeks, like a sulky bulldog.

'I'm one of Joanie's friends.' I had planned to say I was researching former pupils of Hallow's Hill, but it now sounded ridiculous in my head. 'I thought I'd come over, just on the off-chance she was at home.' I cringed at myself, sounding like a child calling in for someone. 'I'm Cameron.'

His face grew even sterner, as his eyes gave me a swift once-over. 'Cameron Morris? Right. Cameron, I kindly ask you to leave us be.'

I pulled the card out of my pocket and held it up. 'Somebody sent this to me. Asking me to stop looking for Joanie.'

His face didn't change, as he replied, 'A Christmas card? I'm kinda in the middle of somethin'. So, if it's alright by you . . .' Before finishing his sentence, he closed the door with a firm nod. Was he angry? Grieving? I couldn't tell. It seemed odd not to answer such a simple question. *Kindly leave us be*, he had said.

Once I was walking towards the local bus station, I looked down at the card again and shuddered in the winter sunshine. *Leave things be. This is a warning.*

Extract from 'Who's Afraid of the Dark?' by Joanie Sinclair, 2012

I had not known a time before this that I was so afraid of the dark. Even as a little girl, I would ride my yellow bicycle around the neighbourhood's streets until the moon shone. In winter, when I was a little older, I would sledge in the pitch black with my school friends on Hallow's Hill.

Now, the dark made me imagine a man in a balaclava coming up the stairs.

21

Joanie, September 2013

One day in late September, Erin invited Joanie to her flat for dinner. The café had become much busier now it was term time, but whenever she had a moment, Joanie would ask David how his research was coming along. In return, he had asked her to read through an article he had written on flora and fauna, as described by Aiden of Maeyar. Her heart had leapt at the mention of the *mergus* as 'most likely a razorbill'.

'I'll be sure to add you to the acknowledgements,' David had said, smiling, when she returned the draft. This was one hundred times better than being thanked for recording a talk.

The evening of the dinner, Joanie thought of Cara as she made her way to the Victorian housing that extended beyond the town's medieval walls. She hoped they could be friends again. Judging by the photographs she posted, Cara was probably too busy to talk to her. *I hope you're OK,* Joanie texted. It was worth a try. *Thinking of you. So much to catch you up on. Turns out Mia works at my café too! Luckily my shifts are with a student guy I kind of like . . .*

Hopefully that would be enough for Cara to start talking to her again.

Erin's address was written on a scrap of paper. It led her to a grey stone terraced house with curling white gables, which sat near the disused railway track that must have been constructed around the same time. She wondered how often she had passed this old street on the way to work and school, without knowing who lived there. She pressed the doorbell to the ground-floor apartment, noticing the long black lines on the stone entrance, where past residents had struck matches for their tobacco pipes before they stepped out into the night.

Erin's head bobbed out of the door. 'Hey!' she said. Her confidence was contagious. The first thing Joanie noticed, as she entered the high-ceilinged hallway, was a sound coming from somewhere inside. It was a low drone, similar to the kind they played in meditation class. The next thing she became aware of was the greenery: a mossy rug over pine floorboards, botanical prints on the walls and tall houseplants pushing past comfortable, if sparse, furnishings. Now she was out of the wind, Joanie's face began to sting. 'Let me take your jacket,' Erin said. 'And sorry to ask this, but can I grab your phone too?'

'Sorry?' Joanie wasn't sure she had heard correctly.

Erin smiled and rolled her eyes. 'I know. David just has a thing about phones. He thinks they're too distracting and has this whole theory . . . Anyway, if you could just leave it here.' She held out a small basket that had been sitting on a table by the door. 'Sorry to ask.' The slow pulse of sound was strangely relaxing, like they were about to get a massage.

Joanie dropped the phone into the basket. Now she thought about it, she had never seen Erin use one. 'Is this David's flat? I thought . . .' Then it hit her: David and Erin lived together. Of course.

'Is Erin trying to steal your phone?' It was Vik, walking out of the kitchen in a baggy Aran cardigan. He sounded in unusually good spirits. 'You know she sells them on the black market?' His whole manner was looser, more relaxed than at work.

'Come and have a seat,' Erin interrupted, guiding them through to the new, open-plan kitchen, with a large table, where wooden chairs screeched against the quarry-tiled floor.

The evening was still bright in the garden, but the room was made darker by the tall flowers that pushed against the windows.

'Hey.' In rolled-up shirt sleeves, David looked ever the academic even now, stirring a pot on the hob.

Erin lifted a small stack of white dishes from the island and started laying them on the table.

'Vik, are you critiquing my phone policy?' David said. 'Sorry if it seems a bit odd, Joanie, I just find them awfully distracting, especially at dinner parties.'

'I should really use mine less,' Joanie muttered apologetically. 'They are a bit addictive.'

'That's why I don't have one at all,' David said. 'Not a mobile at least. Same reason I don't have a TV, really. Vik's making a joke about it, but he's the same way, aren't you, Vik?'

Vik shrugged at Joanie. 'I'm trying it, for a while. He persuaded me.'

She felt a pang of shyness, now they were outside of the café.

'And you admit,' said David, 'it's helped your concentration, your sleep and no doubt your brain cells. Mobile phones, I always say, work in opposition to one's intellect.'

Joanie nodded, wishing she had something insightful to add.

At that moment, there was a loud *pop*. Joanie turned to see Erin uncorking a bottle of champagne.

'Congratulations are in order!' Erin said, filling four glasses and passing them around. 'David's just had some fantastic news.'

'Oh, come on now,' said David. 'It's just some funding.'

'*Just* some funding?' replied Vik.

'So modest,' said Erin. 'It's like *a lot*. A big ass research grant. And for those tiny fragments, too.'

'Well,' said David, 'they're not *tiny*. At least not symbolically . . .'

'*Cheers*, everyone!' Erin exclaimed, cutting him off. As Joanie joined in, smiling, it was the happiest she had felt in a long time.

After the champagne, they took their places at the table, while Erin and David took turns to serve an assortment of baked vegetables and stews.

'Butternut squash and bean gratin. Charred aubergines and courgettes,' said Erin, pointing to each dish in turn. 'Braised cauliflower. It's all vegan.'

'It looks delicious,' said Joanie, with genuine surprise.

As they began to eat, the three academics exchanged departmental gossip, while Joanie followed along with amusement. Vividly told tales about the drunken colleague at a conference; an astonishingly entitled email from a student; how the Medieval Society's last banquet had ended in food poisoning.

Within the walls of his own home, David was a charming yet more introverted host, while Vik became an entertainer, addressing the table with good-natured jokes. Joanie could see they were putting on a show for someone, before realizing it was her.

This was exactly the kind of flat Joanie wanted

to live in when she finally moved away from home. Now and again, she noticed small details in the décor. The artfully arranged piles of books and antique ornaments would have made perfect photos for social media. She wished David wasn't so eccentric about phones.

'I really enjoyed your talk, David,' Joanie said, when the conversation lapsed into silence. 'Super-interesting.'

'Thank you,' he replied. 'In my next one I want to talk about how Aiden of Maeyar, really, was a proto-ethnobiologist.'

'What's that again?' she asked, trying to look interested. 'Erin mentioned the fragments and—'

David smiled generously. 'It's someone who studies how people use plants, like myself. Aiden survived the attack on the monastery on Maeyar and he wrote about it. He noticed that the Norsemen seemed to be in some kind of altered state when they raided. It seemed unholy to him, terrifying. That was when he started to experiment with different combinations of plants to try to figure out what had happened to them. The berserker warrior has been such a mysterious figure. Now I am translating his manuscript for the *very first time* – actually *reading* it for the very first time since it was lost. That's where the fragments come in.'

'And the funding,' said Erin. 'So David can expand his research further. Less teaching, more travel! The manuscript contains so many eye-opening details about who these raiders actually *were*. How they understood the natural world. And religion.'

'I'm planning to write a book on Aiden, too. Like Erin says, he studied plants here and in the north of Scotland and he also, I'm discovering, made predictions about the future. When he started taking these plants, he basically became a pagan. Or, at least, that's the argument I'm making. He didn't eat meat, either, because he was a monk. So that's partly what inspired me to become vegan.'

'Uh – as well as myself,' Erin chipped in.

'Well, thank you, darling. I've found it improves my focus,' David continued.

'You basically want to be him,' said Vik, teasingly.

'What did you mean by him becoming a pagan?' asked Joanie.

'He stopped following the Bible and believed in the power of nature,' said David.

'But . . .' Joanie was confused '. . . what about the Vikings? Didn't they murder all those monks and people? He was OK with that?'

David laughed. 'Not exactly. No, he didn't condone it. He just started writing about it, then became curious about their way of life. He didn't *become* one of them, but he started to find out which plants they used, and that's what I'm most interested in.'

'What kind of plants?' she asked, looking out to the tendrils that pressed against the window.

'Well, we're pretty sure they used henbane, as I spoke about at the library. I'm looking for some volunteers to help me prove this theory. We had a lot of interest after the talk.'

'Volunteers?' asked Joanie. 'To try henbane?'

David laughed. 'Oh, it's a bit more scientific than that. We're still figuring out the details. It used to be a commonly used analgesic for everyday things such as stomach ache, coughs, asthma, that sort of thing. It's a really misunderstood plant. It's linked to the transcendental experience. Like a meditation aid. I think, with more work, we can really harness these findings and re-examine the use of these ancient herbs, even in our everyday lives.'

'Have you tried it?' Joanie asked.

She noticed Vik shift in his seat.

'I've experimented, yes, in small doses. Totally changed my way of seeing the world.'

'I love all of us hanging out like this!' Erin butted in, sounding like she was trying to move the conversation along. 'Joanie, I asked you here with a bit of an ulterior motive,' she said, laughing. 'I'm going up north soon, to David's family's cottage, to further my meditation practice.'

'What she means is, she's skiving off work,' said Vik. 'Baking bread, strolling through fields.' Joanie had not seen this side to him. He was like an annoying big brother.

'Oh my God, Vik, *shut up*. This is a business I'm

running. I have to improve my technique sometimes. I have to practise what I preach,' Erin snapped back, busily gathering up her surfer hair into a messy bun that looked effortlessly chic. 'Anyway, Joanie, I just wondered if you wanted to come with me, up to Caithness. It seems like you're really enjoying the classes. I could teach you and then maybe, maybe, you could take over some of my classes. We could see how it panned out.'

'I'd *love* to!' Joanie flushed with excitement. 'You don't mind, David? Is your family still there?'

'Oh no, it's a holiday let,' said Erin. 'In fact, I was thinking all four of us could go. You're better at driving long journeys than me, Vik. I'm asking some of the new recruits to man the fort.'

Vik caught Joanie's eye and her stomach flipped. 'Sure,' he said. 'I love baking bread.'

'Vik, are you kidding me?' Erin said. 'It's more about experiencing the . . . wilderness. Just being. You know?'

'I think I know what you mean,' Vik said. 'Lounging.'

'David?' Erin asked with an eye-roll. Joanie could tell she secretly loved the way Vik spoke to her.

'Of course,' David replied. 'Nobody's been up there for a while. In fact, I think the site of the Olrich settlement is still there and—'

'OK, OK, can we wrap it up for now with the monk chat?' Erin said.

A look passed between them. David smiled. 'Of course, darling.'

For the rest of the meal, the group spoke about the new local bookshop, Sands & Sons, and how busy the town was. Vik described how much his parents had enjoyed their trip to St Rule last month from India. Joanie noticed he kept looking at her from across the table as he spoke. She looked away, her stomach tight. She wondered whether this was meant to be a double date.

The candlelight was soft on her eyes after the sunshine outside. And without people constantly checking their phones, like her friends, the dinner felt more intimate, even secret.

When David passed Joanie the last of the cauliflower, she noticed an intricate tattoo edging out from under his rolled-up shirt sleeve. A band of runic symbols.

Erin jumped in again, only to tell them it was time for pudding. She brought out a flourless, dark chocolate cake, decorated with violets. Despite her best intentions, Joanie reached for her phone instinctively, only to remember it had been relegated to the hallway. There was no clock in the kitchen, so she had no idea how late it was. Time had seemed to ebb and flow. She could picture herself now, as a student, as a young woman.

When the night finally came to a close, Vik offered her a lift home. She was unsure if he was just being polite, as she sleepily recited her address. The car was old, second-hand but cool and retro. Not what she really expected for a student. He looked much more awake than her in the driver's seat, turning on low indie music. 'Are you going to give up your phone and become vegan too?' Joanie asked.

'Well, what David says goes.' Vik paused. 'He has his ways. He's actually my supervisor, for my PhD. We're friends now and everything, of course. He is just . . .' he thought for a moment '. . . a very *persuasive* man, I would say. He has helped me a lot, in my field of research. Everyone in the department loves him, of course. Some people think he's a genius, in fact. He definitely believes that.'

He spoke with a conspiratorial air, as if they were two outsiders talking.

When he dropped her off at her small, suburban house, Joanie had felt a pang of shame. She wished she lived somewhere big and old like Erin and David. Vik didn't seem to notice. He parked the car to let her out. 'It was nice hanging out. Perhaps you'd like to meet up again. Maybe we could go for a walk on the beach or something.'

'Sure,' Joanie said, trying to sound cool. 'Why not?'

22

Cameron, 27 December 2023

I had booked my train back to London for just after Hogmanay, but was starting to wonder how to fill the time. I had imagined that home would provide a refreshing distraction from my break-up, that I would no longer be someone who wanted to stay in their pyjamas, listening to podcasts and raiding the fridge. Yet there I was in my dressing-gown at eleven a.m., eating salami and cheese on a posh cracker and listening to two comedians discuss the French Revolution.

My mind began to drift. I searched for Joanie's name online yet again. This time, I clicked through friends and places on various social-media sites. Nothing.

Mia had sent me a message: *Hey, great to see you the other night. Any luck finding out what Joanie's been up to? Are you in town for long?*

I clicked on to her profile page and saw the latest photo she had posted was a pile of young-adult novels in front of a fancy bookcase, a ladder to one side. They were the kind of books some of my students liked to read, about dragons and love triangles. Well, she would know about the latter.

I was deciding whether or not to reply when Tatey messaged to say he was waiting outside.

'I knew you'd be in the house,' he said, as I got into the passenger seat. 'I was passing, and I thought, Morris will still be sat on his arse, watching telly, guaranteed.'

'No, I wasn't,' I said. I had been lying down scrolling on my phone.

'Your London pals might think you're this man of the world, Morris, but I know the real you.' He was joking, but I was glad he didn't elaborate further. Nobody thought I was a man of the world. Since breaking up with Vanessa, I barely felt adult enough to be a man.

The van smelt bad. Whether animal, vegetable or mineral, I wasn't yet sure. 'Been up to much?' Tatey asked, backing the van out of the drive.

God, he almost ran over my mum's flowerbed. 'Dunno, really,' I said. 'Ate a lot of Quality Street.'

He gave me a side eye. 'The plot thickens. Now where, in the Kingdom, d'ya want to go?'

I had assumed he had somewhere planned. 'Buddy. The rock,' I said, without thinking. 'How about there?'

'Excellent choice,' he replied, turning towards

Boar's Raik. 'Let's go the scenic route.' It felt like old times again, two inconsequential pricks in a mystery machine.

As we drove, I noticed a small holy figure hanging from his rear-view mirror.

'St Christopher,' Tatey said, as I took a closer look. 'Patron saint of car drivers. I'm not kidding. Also doubles up if you have toothache.'

'I thought he was for lost people,' I said, as he drove along the quiet country road. The barren fields sparkled with frost either side of us.

Tatey shook his head. 'Nah, that's St Anthony. I like St Christopher. Way back, they found a giant tooth that was said to belong to him. A relic. People worshipped it. Turned out to have belonged to a hippopotamus.'

Trust Tatey to know something like that. 'What's St Rule's deal?' I asked. I had never bothered to find out.

'Golfers. Obviously.'

I smiled, but I couldn't quite relax, as my mind wandered back to the Christmas card that had been pushed through my door. Tatey was the only person I could think of who lived nearby.

'Patron saint of fudge doughnuts also, St Rule,' Tatey continued, alluding to a local delicacy.

Could he be hiding something? He didn't seem the sort to send weird messages but you never knew.

'No,' I said, speaking in my teacher's voice, before

I could stop myself. 'A saint has to patronize *someone*,' I say, 'not things.'

'You're doing a pretty good job of that yourself,' Tatey muttered, with his eyes firmly on the road, and we lapsed into silence.

After a while, Tatey put on a classic metal album and the mood changed. I started nodding along, ironically at first, but then I got into it. The lyrics were about lust and magic and shadows. Everything Father Thomas had warned us against. Tatey turned up the volume at the complicated solo. I let out a whoop as he swung round a corner, one hand on the steering wheel. We sped along more winding roads, lost in teenage air guitar, as the December sea dipped in and out of view.

As we started to walk through the field towards the beach, I wondered how many times I had trodden this path. I thought about my dad coming here when he was a boy. And how many others before him? There was a timeless quality. Where the rocky coast met the ocean, I could almost see pagans standing in their white robes against the grey waves, preparing a human sacrifice, with sprigs of mistletoe like the one over our door. Clearly Tatey's choice of music had gone to my head.

We were nearing the edge of the field that ended in a rocky downward path to the beach. 'Do you think there were, like, druids and shit here?' I asked Tatey. If anyone knew, it would be him.

'Druids? Like in *Asterix* times?' he replied.

'Yeah,' I said. That lesser-known time period.

'What was the druid guy called in that?' he asked, as we walked in the cold wind. 'Jetafix?'

I laughed loudly. 'Getafix. Like taking drugs. Maybe a little inappropriate for nine-year-olds.'

Tatey looked at me. 'Like "Get a fix of his magic potions, children"? That's too good, man.'

Now I was on a roll. 'He's called Panoramix in French. Not as good at all.'

'Do you *ever* stop being a teacher? But *Getafix*, man. When were these books written? The swinging sixties?'

'Yep.' I knew my *Asterix*. We had reached the end of the field and were scrambling down the banks to the shore. Buddy the rock was in sight.

Tatey ran out ahead of me. 'The magic potion made them really strong, right?' He threw a stone far into the freezing water, as though hoping for super-strength himself.

I ran against the wind to catch him up, shouting, 'So they could go and beat people up.'

He started galloping across the sand like a fool. 'Like a blind rage . . . roid rage?'

'No, no, don't do that to *Asterix*!' I covered my eyes and fell upon the sand, like an invisible arrow had hit me.

I opened my eyes and Tatey had disappeared.

The frosty beach stretched out around me and I remembered the party, the towering bonfire. My teeth chattered.

I looked up and saw Tatey balancing high on a ledge that jutted out from Buddy. He jumped, hit the sand and sprang up, triumphant. I was at once eighteen and twenty-eight. Someone who had never had a girlfriend and someone who had been a fiancé, even for a brief few months.

When Tatey came over to sit next to me on the sand, he was out of breath.

'Hey,' I said. 'Do you remember that party we had here?'

'Which one?' said Tatey. 'We had a bunch.'

'The one at the end of school. That time Adam Deuchars got off with Mia.'

Tatey was looking out to sea, frowning.

'You remember?'

'I think so,' he said, distantly, then looked at me out of the corner of his eye. 'Then you pissed off to Glasgow.'

The change in tone took me by surprise. 'Yeah,' I said. 'Not much I could do about that, really. I keep thinking about Joanie's mum. Didn't you think that was weird? I wonder where Joanie is, these days.'

He shrugged. 'Search me, man.' I had known Tatey a long time and something was off in his voice. Just a tiny hesitation that echoed to the rocks and back.

I watched him carefully. 'OK. I just thought you might know something.'

'There are no facts,' said Tatey, tilting his head back, 'only interpretations.'

'Let me guess,' I replied. 'Nietzsche.'

He pretended not to hear me.

'Well,' I continued, 'talking of facts, something super-freaky happened on Christmas Day, when my parents were out.'

'Oh, aye?' He sounded interested now.

'This creepy Christmas card came through the door. The message said not to try looking for Joanie.' I sighed. 'I haven't told anyone about it, but it was fucking weird.'

He looked genuinely affronted. 'What the hell? No way. Who would do that?'

I shrugged. 'I'm trying not to think about it too much.'

'Why would they even say that? Were you looking for her?'

'No, not really, I mean . . .' Then it hit me like ice water. 'I was talking to Adam about her. About Joanie. At the drinks.'

'Adam.' Tatey gave me a look that said, *Well, there's your problem, right there.*

'I haven't told my parents. Don't tell them. I'm wondering about telling the police, but I don't even know if they'd take me seriously. The way it was written, it was sort of accusatory, you know. Like

I was the one doing something wrong. What if the police thought that too?'

'Put up cameras,' said Tatey, as if that was the easiest thing in the world. 'In case the guy comes back. Then you've got evidence.'

'Yeah.' I sighed. 'You're probably right.' I got up, shaking sand off my boots. 'Let's go and get some beers at The Boar. My round.'

An Adele song was playing as the barman pulled me more pints. We were about six drinks in between us and it was dark outside. The song was one that Vanessa used to sing when she was processing her invoices. *Chasing Payments*, she called it, and I rolled my eyes every time. In spite of my best intentions, the memory made me miss her. I wasn't even an Adele fan. I liked the way Vanessa sang, though. The way she would wear her glasses when she was working at her laptop. Before I knew it, my phone was out and I was composing a message. It didn't matter that she hadn't replied to my last one. Or that we had blocked each other on social media.

Hey. I'm here if you ever feel like talking about stuff. I resisted pressing 'send'. It wasn't the time. I should just enjoy myself. There was something so cosy about this old drinking hole. As well as serving good local beer, The Boar and Barn even had its own resident dog, an old collie cross, which had wagged his tail enthusiastically when we had arrived, as if – I told myself – he remembered me from years ago. Vanessa would have loved it here.

I set the two beers on our table and asked Tatey an open-ended question about the latest Final Fantasy game, just to distract me, but before I could think better of it, I shoved my hands under the table and pressed 'send'.

'*Mildness*, is what I'm trying to say. The side quests *suck*.' Tatey looked at me emphatically, taking a drink as punctuation.

'I hear you, man,' I replied, a little sloppily. The pub's playlist had changed to a nineties rock ballad. Tatey was a good friend. In my opinion, a good friend is someone you can hang out with for extended periods without wishing you were somewhere else. Being a low-key great hang is a vastly underrated quality. Yet I noticed that no matter how long we talked, he always remained monosyllabic when I mentioned Joanie.

Just then the door opened, and my neighbour Stuart Dunn walked in with two other middle-aged guys I didn't recognize. His front teeth protruded slightly and his face was ruddy. I wondered why my mother had any time for him at all. He gave me a nod and I pretended not to see him. Twat.

My stomach had started to feel bloated by the beer. I'd indulged a bit too much over the past few days. 'Think I'd best be heading off,' I said to Tatey. 'My turn to cook for my parents this evening.'

'Nice one,' he replied. 'Remember to get a camera. Look out for any jakey bastards hanging about the hoose.'

I glanced up at Stuart. He was a middle-class retiree who was as good as teetotal, but something wasn't quite right. I was sure of it.

I took some time to pass by the local Co-op to pick up a few things for dinner. I was making *moules marinière* or, as my dad called it, mussel stew. (If he ever found a particularly big one, he would call it a 'clabby doo'.) I needed some decent white wine and crusty bread. If you couldn't eat mussels by the sea, when could you?

'Something came for you,' my mother told me, as I dumped the shopping bags on the kitchen counter. She handed me an envelope and immediately I knew what it was.

'Must be another Christmas card,' I said, shoving it into my pocket.

I went upstairs to the bathroom to open it. The same wintry scene, the same handwriting.

This is your second warning.
STAY AWAY.

Extract from 'Who's Afraid of the Dark?' by Joanie Sinclair, 2012

The heavy footsteps got louder as they started creaking along the landing. I wanted to silence my body. I wanted my heart to stop beating. I wanted to stop breathing. For my organs to disappear into mist. Instead I was a piece of meat, waiting to be eaten. I'm not here, *I thought.* Don't come into my room.

23

Joanie, September 2013

A couple of days later, Joanie met Vik after her shift. This meeting had played over in her head for three days with a current of anxiety. He greeted her with a cool hug; his grungy vintage clothes smelt of detergent. After such a build-up, it felt anticlimactic. Joanie tried to study his expression from beneath her blue baseball cap: he seemed preoccupied, no longer the joker from the dinner party.

There had been so many things she had imagined them talking about, but now they were walking to the beach all conversation slipped away, like the land into the sea.

'Thanks for the lift the other night,' Joanie said, finally.

'No problem,' he replied, his eyes on the road ahead.

'What you been up to?' she asked, as casually as possible.

'Not much,' Vik replied. 'Been helping David with

this manuscript translation. He does have some lofty ideas about it. We're going on a research trip at the weekend, over to the Isle of Maeyar. He hasn't by any chance talked to you about a seabird, has he?'

Joanie laughed. 'Yes. You guys are such nerds, honestly. I can't believe he's still stuck on that.'

As they turned a corner, a wind-lashed grey obelisk came into view. Joanie had known it all her life, but it appeared only now as something interesting to talk about to this out-of-towner. 'That looks like a war memorial, right?' she said, searching Vik's face in profile, waiting for a reaction. 'It's actually for people who had been burned at the stake. Back in the day.'

Vik laughed. '"Back in the day". The Middle Ages, you mean?'

'Yeah,' Joanie said. 'The martyrs.' All she knew of the martyrs was their burning.

This was clearly Vik's topic. Of course he knew about it. 'It was a kind of war, the Reformation,' he said. 'A war of beliefs.'

'How do you know so much?' Joanie said, nudging him.

'It's my field. Besides, I think that's pretty common knowledge,' he teased back.

She stood for a moment to look at the stone structure. It was imposing, no matter how long you had lived here, looming ten metres tall, overlooking the golden expanse of the South Sands beach.

As they walked side by side, Joanie was acutely aware of her body falling in time with his. They were close, without touching. What did he think of her? He didn't behave like the boys from school. He made her laugh. Did that mean he liked her? He walked with purpose as he spoke at length. 'Everything in this town turns out to be where someone got burned or tortured. Do you find that weird?' he asked. 'Or do you get used to it, you townsfolk? I was walking down by Salvation Street the other day, and someone says to me, "Oh, you do know we are walking the route of the Veiled Nun?" The Veiled Nun!'

Joanie laughed, unguarded for a moment.

'And do you know why she's veiled?' he asked.

Who had he been walking with? Another girl? Mia? She nodded to give the impression that she already knew the story.

'Behind the veil she is bloody mutilated. Mutilated herself for love. Love is very overrated. I blame medieval France.' He was smiling that smile again. Joanie wanted to push him over. They were leaving the old town now, crowded as it was with turrets and steeples and stories. They were out in the open, by the famous golf course that sprawled alongside the wide sandy beach ahead of them, bright and dry.

As they walked closer, Joanie could make out two black dogs running in and out of the waves. A couple in anoraks catapulted tennis balls.

'Are you religious?' Vik asked, prodding her shoulder. 'You look mad at me. Nuns are a touchy subject?'

'Oh my God, Vik, stop it.' She pushed him then, playfully, and he jumped off the high ridge of road on to the beach.

'I'm only asking!' he called up. 'There are so many different kinds of Christians here, man.'

Vik held up his hand for her to leap down with him. *I see*, thought Joanie. His grip felt strong. The sky was clear and blue, and sometimes that was all you could ask for in summer.

'You've got your Baptists, your Quakers,' he said.

'Your candlestick-makers,' Joanie finished, making him laugh this time. *Look at me, on a date*, she thought. She wanted to talk to Cara about this man. Her last messages were still sitting unread.

The beach usually made her feel good. She looked around to check for anyone she recognized from school, but the sand was practically empty, a cream canvas, stretching for miles. She watched two figures walk out of the dunes and on to the beach, a man and a woman.

Vik stuck up his arm to get their attention as he walked towards them, grinning. 'Come on!' he said to Joanie, grabbing her hand again. She squinted, walking closer, to see the square posture of David and the tangled hair of Erin.

'Race you,' Vik said, and sped off up the beach.

Joanie chased after him, her feet slipping in the soft sand. She hated him being just out of reach.

'It was ridiculous,' Erin was saying to Vik, when Joanie caught up. 'Oh, *hey*.'

'Hi,' said Joanie, half-heartedly, raising her hand and panting for breath.

'But you did it?' asked Vik. 'You have them?'

'We *do*.' Erin nodded, smiling.

'Cool,' Vik replied. Joanie looked for any sign that his attitude had changed towards David and Erin, but he appeared as enlivened as he had at the dinner party. She could picture them all, on a Highland road trip, drinking wine into the fire-lit evenings.

'So,' said David, turning to Joanie, 'we're hanging back there, in the dunes. Got quite the set-up already.'

'Check you out,' said Vik. The conversation sounded like an annoying inside joke. The salty wind made Joanie's nose run.

'So glad you could join us.' Erin pushed her hair out of her face lazily. 'We wanted to get to know you more before our trip up north.'

At once, Joanie felt stupid for ever thinking Vik had asked her on a date for just the two of them.

'And for you to get to know us better,' said David, languorously, as they walked to a sheltered spot in the dunes where a floral picnic blanket had been laid. David fumbled with a Thermos of herbal tea.

Vik sat down beside Joanie. 'Too much?' he muttered, in a low voice.

'Erin? No . . .' she began, trying not to sound disappointed. She had been expecting a real, grown-up date, just the two of them. That was what she really wanted, she realized.

'You're doing such an amazing job in the café,' said Erin.

Joanie looked up. All three of them were smiling at her. She nodded. 'Thank you. I like working there. With you guys. I'm so excited for our trip.'

'We do stuff like this, come out to the dunes, to really *connect*,' said Erin.

Nobody said 'the dunes'. It was strange being at the beach with them. She had grown up with this large swathe of water and sand that stretched far away from the town's jagged outline. She didn't have to over-think: the beach was simply *there*, an eternal part of the town and her life.

She looked through their eyes at the long, pale grass. The dark, lapping sea. It was a different, slightly more beautiful place: not her beach, but its identical twin. These people moved differently from the townsfolk, their language elevated, their humour more refined. She wanted to move and laugh like them, clean and attractive. She watched the gestures of their hands, the shape of their mouths as they spoke about medieval history. Erin bitched about Mia, and Joanie laughed at her cruel sense of humour as she pulled her baseball cap a little further over her eyes. A crab tucked away in a different shell, drifting in and out of the conversation.

'We get to chill and, you know, experience nature out here. That's what we're all about. Just feel it,' said David, closing his eyes.

Vik laughed. 'Come on, tell her. We're getting high. You guys never get to the point.'

David was taking something out of his inner pocket. They were smiling at her again.

'Mushrooms. If you didn't know yet,' said Vik.

'I kind of knew,' said Joanie. She hadn't. Her surroundings were so familiar and yet so new.

'Liberty caps,' said Erin. 'I knew you'd be down for this.'

It was her choice to join them. She hesitated for a moment, then accepted the small brown mushroom and put it to her mouth, like a communion wafer. She watched Erin and Vik do the same. She had wanted something to wash away her thoughts and feelings. Those of Adam and, in fact, everything, if just for a while. She wasn't scared. These people didn't need to convince her, but they tried to all the same, in their measured, reassuring way. They were academics. Their knowledge was deep, their interest scientific. They wanted to change the world.

'I'm not participating today,' David said, turning to Joanie, as if she had asked for an explanation. 'The experience is better when there's a guide.' He sounded so uncool. 'And someone needs to drive you guys home.'

He explained that she had nothing to worry about. 'Right now, your body is simply converting psilocybin into psilocin, which has a very similar chemical structure to serotonin, regulating mood, stress, sleep . . .' Something about his voice was lulling. She liked that his corduroy blazer matched the colour of his tortoiseshell glasses.

'That's why this stuff is so interesting to me.' He looked around at the group. 'One thing we have in common is we're all anxious people. I mean, we're *thinkers*. It's kind of an occupational hazard.'

Nobody she had met, not even Mia, talked like this. She wished he'd stop.

'We want to heal. From modern life, the effects of technology,' Erin said.

'Psilocin unlocks something, too, in your receptors,' David continued, looking at Joanie. She could tell he was enjoying this opportunity to explain. 'There's this thing we call the default mode network. Some people would take a tenth of this, three times a week. That tea we had at my house. That had a tiny dose of mushrooms in it.'

'I didn't drink it,' Joanie said, trying to remember what he was talking about. Had Vik? Vik had driven her home.

'People have been doing this since the dawn of time,' David continued. 'That's partly what

I love about my studies. You end up finding out we aren't so different from, say, the druids or the Norsemen.'

David's speech began to slow. Then, with time, she lay down. Summer was ending.

Softly the sand started to breathe. She swept it up slowly and let it fall in a golden veil. The grains glittered through her fingers and ran over her arms like friendly ants.

'We like to lie in a circle, like this,' Erin said, reaching for Joanie's hand. Vik took her other hand and lay down too. Distantly, David carried on talking and the sensation of the wind became visible, carrying a bird up high. Joanie watched the bird hover and its sharp eyes watched her.

Joanie understood the breathing classes now. They inhaled and exhaled together as they had practised. She breathed until her body was simply shifting air. Her lungs grew and shrank against the bones of her chest. She was sharing breath between the sand and the sky. Her heart was so present in her body, her blood the rush of seawater. Her capillaries tiny threads of seaweed, gently shivering.

Joanie's hands moved back through the sand, feeling the tiny shell grains. Over and over they stroked the hair of her arms. Through a hilly desert, the deep blue rippled and shone. David was asking her how she felt, but she couldn't answer. The sky was too liquid and beautiful.

This place, this spot, had always been here. The world had always been like this.

With time, the fibrous dune grass grew steadily taller. It was the long hair next to her face, pushing upwards instead of down. The slow voices of her friends asked questions. Their worlds did not match hers. Erin was getting up and running to the churning water, her breath heavy, her bare feet changing the ground. Her gasps were waves of air.

Vik's body moved close to hers on the sand and they stared into each other's eyes. Then his mouth was on hers and they were kissing, his breath hot, his lip piercing, pressing into her skin. She had always wanted this. The kiss reverberated into the pink sky.

24

Cameron, 28 December 2023

A day later, in that strange no man's land between Christmas and New Year, I found myself travelling in the back seat of a car to a party. My sister Kirstin had been invited by her ex-classmate Theo and had come back for the evening, fully recovered from her illness. She was a reassuring presence, her excitement at a night out almost palpable. Her friend Alison was driving and they started to gossip about people I vaguely remembered from school. Sitting there, watching the dark, rainy farmland zip by, I was a little brother, tagging along uninvited.

The party was at a large house in the countryside. Theo's mother greeted us at the door. I looked through at the busy hallway, where people my parents' age were talking animatedly in well-tailored outfits, wine glasses in hand. A younger version of myself would have resented these genteel surroundings, but now the place felt oddly welcoming.

'I think Mum and Dad should have come,' I said

to Kirstin, who had made a beeline for the canapés next to the kitchen dresser.

'I did ask them.' She helped herself to a blini. Typical behaviour.

A familiar North American voice cut through the crowded kitchen. It set my teeth on edge. 'Are those Tunnock's Teacakes over there? It's been a *very* long time since I had one of those.' It was Adam again, lucky me.

'Are they your Proustian madeleine?' asked a man with a clipped Edinburgh accent, wild greying hair and an artfully dishevelled suit.

'My what-now?' Adam asked charmingly. He was wearing a fleece like it was a dinner jacket. I seemed to remember he had a brother in Kirstin's class.

'It's a taste that evokes your childhood,' I replied, a little too loudly, slipping into French-teacher mode. 'Like the ending of *Ratatouille*.'

Adam didn't look very impressed by my helpful Disney comparison.

'*Très bien!*' the older man exclaimed at me, existing – presumably – in a permanent state of academia. 'Did you know, it only became a madeleine on the third draft of *À la Recherche*. It was, at one point . . .' he paused to pop a mini quiche into his mouth '. . . a *biscotto*.'

'Every day's a school day,' Adam said, looking around for someone less eccentric to talk to, which at this party presented a bit of a challenge. 'I'm in tech.'

'I'm a French teacher,' I said, ignoring him. The acoustics in the kitchen were starting to hurt my ears. 'I'm always telling my A-level students to read just a little Proust, even if it's in English.' God, I sounded like a wanker. I hadn't read Proust since uni. I could sense Adam looking around the room and sloping off, while this man talked to me about a paper he had written: *Involuntary Memory and the Madeleine*. His teeth were yellow. The way he smelt reminded me of nicotine and mouldy roses. Kirstin had disappeared into the crowd.

I spent most of the evening talking to kindly parents of friends, and academics who were keen to tell me about the books they were writing and research they were conducting. I was happy to listen and gain insight into their esoteric worlds. It was enviable, actually. I started to entertain the idea that I could do a PhD, like Mia. Maybe I would stop brushing my hair and start wearing floral shirts or black polo necks. Every now and then I would see Adam's head in the crowd and feel the inexplicable compulsion to talk to him.

The party turned out to be much more fun than I had anticipated: folk from school and their parents having an unexpected blast in the middle of nowhere. It was only after the clock had struck midnight, after Kirstin's friend had played the bagpipes on the curving staircase, after the impromptu ceilidh dancing in the hall, after the whisky cocktails in the teapot, that I gained the courage to speak to Adam again.

We were standing by a slightly lopsided bookcase in the living room. I took a quick glance at a shelf that seemed to be dedicated to Danish philosophers. Cushions, blankets, lampshades and rugs made a bohemian patchwork around us. Guests were starting to leave, red-faced from good wine.

'You get your Tunnock's?' I asked.

'Ha! Oh, yes. It's good to be back,' he replied, scanning the other people in the room, as though he, too, was looking for someone. 'You forget so much.' The North American accent sounded softer now and his eyes had started to droop.

I cleared my throat. 'I was kinda hoping I'd bump into Joanie,' I said, waiting to see his reaction. I was sure he knew where I lived.

He did a sort of Gallic shrug and drank from the paper cup he was holding.

I pressed on: 'Have you seen her about much?' The question sounded ridiculous; I was aware of that, but didn't care.

He looked performatively confused. 'Have I seen her about? Here?'

'Or, you know,' I said, 'after we left school.'

'You asked me the same thing at the pub.' He sounded annoyed now. 'I went to Canada, and that was kinda it, ya know? It's been such a long time. That's all I can really say.'

I studied his face as he spoke. In the dim light of the room, he looked gaunt, his deep-set eyes in shadow. I wanted to ask about the Christmas cards, but I knew it wouldn't go down well. Maybe it would create a scene, just as people were starting to leave.

Another question slipped out instead. 'Was it awkward seeing Mia at the pub?' I still felt a latent anger for the way he had betrayed Joanie, all those years ago.

He let out a short, surprised laugh. 'You mean, after what happened? God, no one would let me live it down. Even now. That night was stupid. Really *stupid*. OK? God. You must have seen how *out* of it we both were. She had smoked too much and she was just *very* . . . insistent. That girl was . . . trouble. I know that's not cool to say, these days, but it's true. Seeing her again, the other night, I don't know what I was thinking.' He dropped his voice and leaned in. 'I didn't know how much she hated Joanie until afterwards. It was like she was trying to hurt her through me. What do they say? It's always the quiet ones?'

He made it sound like she had manipulated him. I tried to replay seeing them, but the night was too blurry, over a decade ago. Perhaps I had had a sinking feeling when they had gone off together. Still, something didn't feel quite right here. I couldn't put my finger on it. 'So, you don't come back so much?' I asked.

'A couple of times, over the years, but I guess I don't feel the need to,' he replied, taking another swig and suppressing a burp. 'I mean, is that surprising, given what I just said? I sense you don't come back much either. Work is good and I have some family there. And, well, I'm getting married later this year. She's Canadian. This will be my last Christmas trip alone.'

'Congratulations,' I muttered, with as much sincerity as I could muster.

We stood awhile in silence. At one end of the room, a large oak fireplace glimmered with fairy lights. Its mantelpiece was filled with Christmas cards. I scanned them, looking for a snowy field with a rabbit, but there wasn't one. A tree, laden with silver stars, stood in a corner of the room. One of my mother's paintings, I noticed now, hung on another wall. Two crabs on a table, facing each other.

I could hear goodbyes in the hallway. I thought Adam was about to leave too, when he spoke again. 'I hear you're getting married too. Congratulations.' He was nodding and smiling, but the smile didn't meet his eyes.

'Who told you that?' My throat felt dry.

'Oh, just people, you know,' he said, sounding Canadian again and gesturing to the emptying room. 'Your sister.'

'Fucking hell,' I said, pinching the bridge of my nose. 'The family rumour mill.' It was time for me to be getting home. 'Gotta find Kirstin, now you mention her,' I said, turning to leave, with a feeling of relief. 'Good to catch up.'

'Did you have a thing with Joanie?' he asked, as I was about to walk away. 'It's all in the past so you can be honest with me. Is that why you're bringing this up?'

I shook my head, staying rooted to the spot. 'It's just funny. Nobody I speak to seems to know where she is.'

'Or maybe they just don't want to tell you.' He laughed and started to walk off, placing his empty glass on one of the bookshelves. How thoughtful.

'If you're the guy,' I said, looking at him intently as he turned his back, my words slurring slightly from nerves or drunkenness, I wasn't sure which. 'If you're the guy . . .' He was already away. I dropped my voice. 'You will live to regret this.'

Extract from 'Who's Afraid of the Dark?' by Joanie Sinclair, 2012

There was silence, for a while. I don't know how long. I hoped that, somehow, he had disappeared. A ghost. Maybe my house was haunted.
   Then a beam of torchlight slid under the door.

25

Joanie, September 2013

Things were different after the mushrooms on the beach. Joanie couldn't stop thinking about Vik. Her anxiety was replaced by a more positive twin, an energy that made her twist her hair around her fingers as she stood in the empty café, waiting for something to happen.

How's it going with the café guy? Cara texted. Joanie's heart leaped. So much time had passed that she had wondered whether they would ever talk again. Nevertheless, she had been following Cara's life through a steady stream of social-media posts. Each image was like a postcard from another universe.

Joanie checked her phone. Cara's last post was a tousled selfie in which she was squinting into a camera flash. Cameron liked every photo Cara posted, Joanie noticed. Sometimes he would leave cringy little comments in French. Under the latest, Joanie typed: *We get it, Cameron. You're getting ready for your French degree.* Then she deleted her reply, thinking better of it. She had seen him once as she was walking to work: he was getting into a car in town. Before she could wave hello, she had felt an inexplicable pang of shame about the party and turned sharply into a side-street to avoid him. Looking at his profile, she saw something about his new job at a pub in Dundee. And, not that she was keeping track, it looked like something was going on between him and the awful girl he had been talking to at the beach. Mia's friend, Chloë. *She* must have been the reason he didn't warn her about Adam.

And, in terms of Cara's question, how *was* it going with Vik? She liked the fact that he didn't know anything about her. He didn't have social media.

Not much to report, Joanie replied, *but we might have had a moment . . .*

She didn't want to speak too soon. When their shifts overlapped, they smiled at each other like before, but didn't talk much, beyond polite conversation. She was waiting for him to say something more, to progress whatever was going on between them. She didn't want to look desperate. Besides, the café had grown a lot busier in the past few days now that the students were back. As she served drinks, their kiss had replayed in her head over and over, in saturated 1950s technicolour. Had the kiss been real? Had it counted?

*

One Wednesday morning in mid-September, a text popped up on her phone that had been sent in the early hours of the morning.

Adam.

Hey, I hope you're doing well. I'm on my way over to visit my folks. Would be great to talk to you.

Joanie didn't know how to feel. A pang of longing was quickly replaced by anger. It was too late: she had moved on. Maybe things would have been different if he had phoned her with an apology several months ago. He was on his way over anyway? How convenient. She couldn't stop rereading the message, unsure how to reply.

Then, just as she was getting ready for work around noon, Adam started to call her. She let it ring out. Another text popped up. *Am in town, you about? X*

She decided she wouldn't reply; he was making her late for work.

As she hurried through the entrance to the quad, she bumped into Vik walking the other way, his leather book bag slung across his body. All thoughts of Adam disappeared.

His smile made her breath quicken. In fact, she barely registered his words when he said, 'Mia's gone.'

'What?'

He moved closer, repeating the words, whispering them into her ear.

Instinctively she threw her arms around his neck. He drew his face close to hers and they moved into a doorway. Their kiss was hungry, her body hot and charged against his. They left with their eyes to the ground, smiling, Joanie to the café and Vik to the library. For the next couple of hours, the incident buoyed her, like a balloon. She reapplied her lipstick in the toilet, wanting more.

'Mia has gone, it's true,' said Erin, when Joanie found the right moment to quiz her. 'Before you ask, I don't know why.'

That just didn't feel believable.

'There's something else,' Erin said. 'A note came for you.'

Joanie's stomach sank. Surely not. Reluctantly, she unfolded the piece of lined paper, torn from a notebook. A message read, *I'm back home for a while. I need to see you. Adam.* His scrawled handwriting seared into her eyes. She read it again. There was no apology.

'He came into the café?' Joanie asked Erin, who was making tea at the counter.

'I don't know,' Erin said. 'It was just lying here, when I arrived.'

Joanie's hand was shaking as she held the note. How did Adam even know she was here? Surely Mia hadn't told him. Adam could have texted her. Something about the physical object invading her space was unsettling. She remembered the way that, at school, he had sometimes passed her a note in the corridor. Those moments had brightened her day, but now they made her shudder. She looked out of the window at the empty quad. She ripped the note in half and threw it into the bin.

When Joanie left the café to go home for the day, she heard her name being called from across the road. She looked over to see Adam, standing there in flesh and blood and board shorts, waving at her solemnly. Her heart pounded as she started to walk away.

He called her name again, then ran over, narrowly dodging a passing car.

Joanie felt numb, looking up at him, waiting for him to speak.

'Hey,' Adam said, in his deep voice. There was a determined look in his eye. He put his hand on her arm and she pulled it away. His body was so familiar to her, yet this was horrible. They stood staring at each other in silence. He tried to smile at her, which enraged her. Apart from some stubble, he looked the same as ever. His annoyingly wide eyes. The irritating jawline.

'What is it?' asked Joanie. She looked around for anyone they might know. 'Why are you here?'

'You got my note?' With his long hair, he looked like an ex-member of a boy band who had learned to surf. 'I tried to call.'

Joanie shrugged.

'Like I said, I'm back for a few days to see my folks and it got me thinking. I just want to talk to you.' He smiled at her hopefully. He had two pointed canine teeth that had always added a wolfish touch to his angelic face.

'No,' said Joanie. 'I don't want to.' She didn't need this. Not when her life was starting to take shape again.

'Please,' said Adam, edging even closer. 'It's important.'

The practised, pleading smile again. She knew it too well. He would use it when he wanted money, cigarettes or beer. Joanie sighed, closing her eyes. She knew when he wanted something he didn't give up. 'I can talk for ten minutes. Then I've got to get home.'

'Altman's? It'll take *five* minutes.'

'Sure.'

Altman's was nostalgic and welcoming, a place her friends used to go to play darts. As soon as they entered, she realized it was not the right setting for an uncomfortable conversation. It held so many good memories and she didn't want to taint them. She started to feel hot, even as they descended into the cool cellar bar. As they looked for a table, she recognized her neighbour Sarah Donaldson, Graham's sister, pulling pints. Joanie slid, head dipped, into a booth.

Adam brought her a Diet Coke from the bar. The ice cubes clinked against the glass as he pushed it towards her. She pretended she hadn't seen it, hating that he knew what she liked to drink without asking. The folk music that pumped from the speakers sounded infuriatingly happy.

'Is there something interesting on that wall?' Adam asked, in the voice he used when he expected a laugh.

Joanie turned to him, her eyebrows raised. Looking at him was hard. As hurt as she felt, she still noticed the perfect proportions of his face. This beautiful man had found her lacking. Was that to be expected?

'Look,' he was saying, in an affable tone, 'I get that you don't want to talk to me. You made that pretty clear. You didn't answer any of my messages, so I didn't really have a choice but to come and find you.'

Whenever Joanie began to soften, an image of his half-naked body on top of Mia's lurched back into her mind's eye. 'How *did* you find me?' she asked flatly.

It was his turn to look away, scratching his neck. Clearly, it was a question he didn't want to answer.

'Are you still in touch with Mia?' she asked, not giving up.

'*No*. No-no-no.' He waved her question away like a politician. He sighed. Subject closed. 'As you don't have much time, I just wanted to tell you. I was drunk. I admit that.'

'Why, though?' Joanie asked, her voice quiet. 'Why her?' This was something that had plagued Joanie since the moment she had found them. Mia was the last person she would have expected him to go for. She was so deeply uncool. Even in her wildest moments of self-loathing, Joanie knew she was more attractive than Mia. Mia didn't wear any makeup or even style her hair most days. How could it have happened?

He shrugged, somewhat theatrically. 'People make mistakes, don't they? It was a big mistake.' He took her hand across the table and she pulled it away. He carried on talking, regardless. 'The long and short of it is, I just want to be with you.' He grabbed her hand again and this time gripped it tightly. 'You need to come back to Canada with me. You'd love it there.'

'Adam, let go.' His hand had held hers a thousand times. It was painful to ask him to stop.

He dropped it, then looked at her, his head cocked to the side. 'Can we at least be friends again? This has been such a tough time. For both of us.'

Joanie's stomach twisted. '*What?* You're not going to apologize?'

He looked deep into her eyes, hands wrapped around a pint of IPA. 'I just want to forget about that night, to be honest with you. It was so stupid. But obviously I'm sorry. Very sorry.'

Stupid. The sex was stupid. She wanted to kick him under the table. Instead, she looked at the half-melted ice cubes floating in her Diet Coke and gave them a swirl. 'I spoke to Mia. I don't think you're telling me everything. I think you're still in touch, for one thing. How else could you have found me?' She wasn't sure she believed Mia, but wanted to gauge his reaction.

'What are you doing speaking to her? It's a small town. It wasn't hard to find out where you were.' He was gulping his drink, still looking at her intently.

'I can't believe you think I'd follow you to Vancouver.'

He wiped his mouth with the back of his hand. His expression hardened. 'Mia's lying. Take it from me.'

Joanie laughed sarcastically, 'Oh, you'd *know* about lying, wouldn't you? Better than anyone.' The sand dunes, the stars. That moaning noise.

Adam looked frustrated. 'Don't be like that, Joanie. Don't be petty.' He looked around the empty bar, lowering his voice. 'I'm trying to tell you, my *girlfriend*, that I . . . I *love* you.' He leaned forward as she finally took a sip of her drink. 'I think what we had was pretty fucking special, don't you? I mean, I don't think we're going to get much better than this.'

Joanie almost spat out some Coke. *Than this?* She looked at him, remembering how she had felt when he had kissed her for the first time. *Gratitude.* She had never been able to articulate it before now but she had been grateful for his attention. And he had enjoyed her gratitude, even expected it. He had changed how the rest of the year had seen her. It was true that she had never been a geek, not like Mia, but she hadn't been anything special. He had made it clear what he liked her to wear. He used to tell her, even bought her clothes. Somehow she had felt the pressure to lose weight, to wear more makeup. She hadn't wanted to admit it at the time. To try to keep his attention, while he spent time with other girls. It wasn't going to get much better than *that*?

'I'll take my chances, Adam,' she replied, getting up from her seat. She didn't look back, as she made her way up the stairs and out of the pub, her pulse racing.

The next day was Thursday. In the evening, Joanie went to the meditation class in the library as she usually did. Lines from her conversation with Adam had been flying around her head all day. Each word made her feel angry. She wondered if she had overreacted. She knew if she told her mother what had happened that that would be the conclusion her mum would come to.

She wanted to talk to Cara about it, but her friend hadn't replied to her last message about Vik and she didn't want to bother her. She could see online that Cara's life was busy. She tried to make it seem glamorous, but looking after three children must be exhausting.

Joanie took a deep breath and lay down on her side, towards the back of the room. She felt so tense that the hard floor was oddly welcome on her muscles. Erin was handing out blankets. She heard footsteps and saw Vik's socked feet saunter past her. She turned on to her back and watched him move towards the front and lie down without looking around. She pretended she hadn't seen him either. Then she closed her eyes, waiting for the class to start, trying to be in the moment, trying to quieten her mind.

After a few minutes, she heard someone else lie down beside her, their feet scuffing the floor. She sensed it was someone big, too close. She opened her eyes in the dim light and saw that the man looking back at her, unsmiling, was Adam.

'*Jesus.*' Her voice was a whisper in her dry throat.

He turned on his back, nonchalantly, gazing up at the ceiling. A smile barely visible.

She bolted upwards and started to gather up her jumper and shoes, her face flushing. She dared not look back at Adam or anyone who might be staring at her as she pushed her way out through the heavy doors. Was the guy trying to intimidate her? Was this a joke to him? She started along the gravel path to get as far away as possible from the town.

A man's voice called her name in the cool evening air.

She spun round to see Vik walking towards her, his shoes still undone, his face full of concern. Tears stung the corners of her eyes.

'Are you OK?' He came closer, touching her arm, gently.

'Can we just get out of here?' she asked.

26

Cameron, 29 December 2023

It was nearly the end of the year and I didn't know what I had to show for it. I thought I had only had a few drinks at the party the night before, but my head felt surprisingly fuggy. That morning, I sat at the old desk in my former bedroom and opened my leather-bound notebook, the Christmas present from my parents, intending to make a list of new-year resolutions on its generously sized pages.

The two small Christmas cards fell out from inside the cover. I had forgotten I had tucked them in there when I had come home from the party, still thinking about Adam. The only resolution I wanted was to find out who the hell had sent them. I wrote out a list of people. *Tatey? Adam D? Joanie's stepdad?*

I opened the yearbook again and gazed at Joanie's photo, imagining what she would look like now. Strangely, I remembered spending too long staring at the back of her head through hours of history class. Once or twice, her long, tawny hair had accidentally brushed my hand when she leaned back in her chair.

One time I had even come close to kissing her at a party, unbelievably. It had been at someone's house near Boar's Raik, and they had had a trampoline in the garden. Everyone had been taking turns to come out and jump on it until, for some reason, they had all gone back inside, and it had just been the two of us there, drunk and laughing, lying on our backs. I had moved my body closer to hers and propped myself up on one arm. Can anyone really remember the words that are said before you kiss for the first time? In films, the guy always says something super-smooth, something that makes the girl draw closer as she replies. Maybe I had tried something like that. I'm sure I did. It was the perfect moment. 'I've gotta go,' Joanie had said softly, bringing her face up to mine, before running back into the house.

Taking a deep breath, I got up from the desk in my bedroom and went downstairs to make eggs and bacon for Kirstin and my parents. I drank several cups of coffee, which made me even more jittery. Whenever I felt on edge, a walk on the beach always helped. And I didn't want to go back to London without visiting the South Sands.

My mother said I could use her car. I put the notebook into my backpack, turning over the list of suspicious characters in my mind. As I backed out of the drive, there was Stuart Dunn again, waving at me from the pavement. I wound down the window. His eyes reminded me of a woodland creature's: small and beady underneath tufted grey eyebrows.

'How are you keeping, Cammy?' he asked, leaning through the window, smelling of stale tobacco. Only my mother called me Cammy.

'Alright, yourself?' I had places to be.

'We're having a wee get-together for Hogmanay at ours, just a few drinks. Do tell your mother. And father.' He smiled, but his eyes stayed beady.

'Will do. See you now!' I said cheerily, decisively pressing the window button. I would conveniently forget that invitation.

By the time I arrived in St Rule, the day was getting on and the light was faltering. The old grey town was quiet, with just a few people out shopping as I walked along Martyr's Street. Despite the coffee, tiredness was creeping up on me and I started to feel lightheaded. I drifted past the glowing shop fronts and realized I was automatically making my way to Alan's Fish Bar. The town chippy. It brought back memories of being crammed into Cara's green Beetle on the way to yet another house party, rain pummelling the roof as indie bands played from a cassette adapter. I had even queued there with my dad on hot days when I was young enough to be holding a bucket and spade.

In London fish suppers were rare to come by.

When you found one, it was usually a slimy imitation with a side of skinny French fries that went cold before you had left the shop. Fife, with its network of coastal villages and potato fields, produced the best there was and we knew it.

When I reached the right street corner, my heart sank to see a new, shinier storefront in its place. Grey Fryer's Fish, the sign read. I rolled my eyes and scanned the menu outside. Maybe I wasn't one to talk with my *moules marinière*, but 'bougie' didn't begin to cover it. The sound of 'black pudding popsicles' gave me the boak. Tourist money had always kept the town afloat, but this was getting ridiculous. From the small crowd of customers inside, it did look popular, however.

As I went in grudgingly, to buy something to eat, I glanced up at the chip shop's mirror and caught a man's eye in the queue behind me. He was thirty-something, wearing a blue baseball cap and seventies-style coat. A piercing glinted on one side of his lip. Not your average golfer.

I hastily looked away and yet, as I placed my order, I could have sworn he was still staring at me.

I had to admit the haddock was good, very good, if much more expensive than before. I started to make my way towards the beach through St Rule's wiggly streets. The light was disappearing. A couple of students passed me as I walked. They always looked so healthy, their cheeks pink from Frisbee-throwing or hours on the golf course. This wasn't term time, so there were far fewer of them around as I left the shelter of the town, with its turreted, baronial architecture, and arrived at the tarmacked road to the beach. I had learned to drive on that road, in that sprawling, sandy car park, its seagrass flattened from years of tyres.

As soon as I heard the sea, my whole body relaxed. In the greying light, I jumped down from the road on to the beach. Something about the activity, putting one foot in front of the other in the wide, empty space, felt cleansing. I looked back at the town, where lights were beginning to come on. I had been doing this for most of my life. I had spent summers here as a child, building sandcastles and braving the cold tides. Today the sea was dark and amorphous, the slate sky melding with miles of sand.

I turned my head and caught sight of the man in the baseball cap again, walking further down the beach behind me. He strode evenly, with purpose. People came here to amble by the shore, walk their dogs or play some kind of sport. There was nowhere to go, except back the way you came.

I felt clumsy trying to eat my chips and walk at the same time, so I sat down by the dunes to my left and stared out at the sea, waiting for the man to pass. He never did. When I stood up to head back to town, I couldn't see him. I told myself he was allowed to follow the same route as me in this tiny town. Perhaps he had been going back to the car park. All the same, I kept looking over my shoulder into the falling dusk.

Extract from 'Who's Afraid of the Dark?' by Joanie Sinclair, 2012

The door squeaked and started to open. Gloved fingers curled round it. A hand large enough to be a man's. The torchlight swung like a lighthouse beam, blinding me.

27

Joanie, September 2013

Vik's flat was a short walk from the café, in another converted Victorian terrace, near the School of History, upstairs this time. Joanie could hear the sea outside as they entered his living room. The place was spartan, but elegant: its corniced white ceiling flowed into a large bay window that framed the night sky. The bare wooden floorboards were scattered with all sorts of tech flotsam and jetsam. Mixing decks, wires, speakers. 'Excuse the mess,' he said. *My flatmate*, he mouthed, pointing his thumb to the kitchen next door, where a kettle was boiling. A man came through, holding a mug of tea, and introduced himself as Joshua, a politics student from Singapore, while trying to hide his puzzlement as to what Joanie was doing there.

'I thought you'd be in bed by now!' Vik said, joking.
'Assignment deadline. It's not going well.' There was an awkward silence. 'So,' he couldn't resist asking, 'how do you guys know each other?'

'We work at Hallowed Ground,' Vik replied. 'I'm sure I told you.'

Joanie was sure he hadn't. It stung, even after Joshua had left the room.

'Is everything OK?' Vik asked. He had asked the same question on the way to his flat.

Joanie could only give the same answer as she had then. 'Did you see that guy who lay down next to me? He's my ex-boyfriend. Over from Canada. He just turned up at the class. I told him yesterday I didn't want to see him any more.' She paused. 'We broke up because of Mia,' she said quietly. 'That's why she always made me so anxious.'

He looked genuinely shocked. 'He sounds like a weirdo,' said Vik, trying to cheer her up with his awkward humour. 'They both do.' He pulled her in for a hug and kissed her head protectively. At once, Joanie relaxed as she began to kiss him back.

Soon they sat entwined, in comfortable silence, listening to the waves outside. Joanie took in more of her surroundings. A record collection. Textbooks. A vintage map on the wall. Vik asked her if she was hungry. He would order something. He started dialling a number on a landline.

'I don't know anyone who has an actual landline still,' she said.

'It makes my life easier,' said Vik. 'I save a lot of money.'

'So that's why you never gave me your number,'

Joanie said, trying to sound like she was joking.

'You can have my number any time you want.' He pretended to look annoyed. 'But I want you to try and remember it. Not put it in your phone, like everyone else. Nobody knows anyone's number any more.'

Joanie thought about how, when she was a child, she could recite her three best friends' numbers off by heart. 'Only if you remember mine,' she said to him.

While they waited for the pizza to arrive, they listened to a record player, old bands that Joanie hadn't heard of, and repeated each other's numbers, like they were the lyrics to a song.

'You're strange,' said Joanie, giving Vik another kiss. 'Do you know that?'

'It seems you like weird guys,' he said.

She bristled. 'What's that meant to mean?'

'Oh, come on, I was joking.'

Joanie went to the window. 'I think I can see our pizza.'

'Don't tell Erin we got the extra mozzarella,' said Vik. 'She's trying to make me vegan too.'

He came over and put his arms around her again. 'I like you,' he said. 'I want you to know that. I also want to say that I'm not going to come on the trip with you guys.'

'Oh. Why not? Is it Erin?' Joanie asked, narrowing her eyes as her heart sank. 'David?'

The doorbell rang and Vik left to fetch the pizza.

When he came back and opened the hot box on the table, he said, 'It's not Erin. It's really a work-related thing. David and I had a bit of a disagreement over the manuscript he's working on. It was hard to talk about. He's my supervisor, as I think I've told you. And he's been super-helpful. You remember he was talking about the manuscript at his house? I won't get into the details, but it's just not a good time for me to go.' He sighed, then started to speak again. 'Recently, I went with him and some other students to Maeyar. The island. He wanted to experiment. With drugs, of course. Kind of like at the beach. But it was different. There were these tourists, for one thing.' He laughed. 'They have a visitor centre.'

'Yes, I know,' said Joanie, a little too sharply. 'I used to work there. Did I not tell you?' She tried hard to remember if she had ever seen Vik before. There had been so many tour groups, coming and going. David's face was familiar, but Vik's she would have remembered.

'Well, it ended on a bad note. I'm not really interested in doing that again.'

'But that's not why we're going. It's not for his research; it's a trip with me and Erin. We're doing breath stuff. Meditation. It's not Maeyar, it's a cottage in the Highlands. Come on. You and me can drive up?' She blinked at him, pleadingly. 'It'll be so fun.'

'Well. There was something else I wanted to tell

you. I applied for a visiting studentship. I thought there was no chance in hell I'd get it. But, er, I recently found out I've been accepted.'

'OK...'

'It's in Bologna.'

Joanie's stomach dropped. 'What?' She wasn't sure she'd heard correctly.

'Don't be too effusive.'

'I'm sorry,' said Joanie. 'I just... wasn't expecting you to say that. Is that in Italy?'

He smiled in a way that annoyed her deeply. 'Yeah, it's only the oldest university in the world. One of the few older than this place.'

Maybe that was why he'd been a little hot and cold. 'OK. Well done. I really mean that. I don't know what a visiting studentship is, but it sounds fancy. I'm guessing you'll be away for a while. Why the hell are you telling me right now? You knew I was upset!'

'I only just found out. I'll be there for the best part of a year. I have to move there. I applied because I really needed to get out of St Rule and... well, I wasn't expecting to meet you. I'm sorry.' He scratched his head, with a grimace. 'I really like you.'

Joanie bit into a slice of pizza thoughtfully. The hot stringy cheese scalded the roof of her mouth. The news was too sudden, too much. She'd get the bus home. How did Vik get to travel abroad but she couldn't even make it out of St Rule? She wanted him to miss her. She wanted him to need her in his life. But perhaps she was wanting too much. Things seemed to be moving too fast. It would be good to go away for a little bit, to gain the space and time to think and breathe.

28

Cameron, 30 December 2023

The following afternoon I drove to a newly refurbished pub that had caught my eye in St Rule to spend a couple of hours reading one of my dad's detective novels. It felt nice to do something for no other purpose than enjoyment. I could nurse a pint without any pressure to buy another. I had even started to think about moving back up north for good.

At about five p.m., the street outside was as dark as night and I decided to make my way back to the car park. The temperature had dropped, and somewhere in the distance bagpipes were playing. I remembered the young man at the party, two nights before, descending the staircase, playing 'Auld Lang Syne'. I didn't recognize this music, which sounded more sombre as it echoed through the town's shadowy, medieval roads. As I made my way further along the cobbles of Martyr's Street, I saw firelight moving towards me, like a glowing river. The main road had been closed off and a line of students, in their long purple gowns, was headed this way. It seemed the university was coming alive again, before term had even begun. An early start to our new-year celebrations.

Shoppers bundled up in scarves and puffer jackets began gathering either side of the road, as the gowned procession came closer. The lit torches cast shadows over young faces. The students walked slowly, without talking, careful not to extinguish the precariously wild flames that burned at the tops of heavy wooden poles. They were moving in the direction of the harbour. More people – locals and tourists – came out of pubs and shops to gather at either side of the road, taking out their phones to record the spectacle.

Like many of the university's bizarre traditions, the meaning of this ritual eluded me. I had no more idea of why the students were solemnly processing than why, when term started in the autumn, crowds of them ran riot in the town, dousing each other with water, flour and foam until they were a seething white mass. In spring, they processed in historical costume, led by a carriage bedecked with flowers, while a male student in a white dress and wig leaned out of the window and waved. Nothing like that happened in the urban campuses of Edinburgh or Glasgow. Smaller and more rural, St Rule was a law unto itself.

As more spectators started to gather around me, waiting for the students to pass, I noticed the man from the beach on the other side of the street, frowning at me in his fashionable coat. Just then, the bagpipes grew louder and the procession moved between us, the bright torchlight demanding my attention. When I squinted at the other side of the road, the man had disappeared.

Alarmed, I made my way through the crowd and ducked down a side-street, unsure where to go. Ahead of me lay a few shops set into the Georgian architecture. They were all closed, apart from one, the glowing town bookshop, Sands & Sons. I looked over my shoulder. There was no one else on the street. It was late afternoon and a few people milled about inside. I pushed my way through the door into warmth and brightness, and the outside world turned black. Wooden ladders leaned against the shelves here and there, inviting someone to climb them, while alcoves revealed comfy armchairs and dangling house plants. As I moved further inside, away from the window, I saw that a few customers were seated among cushions, monstera leaves and small pots of tea.

My mind spun as I browsed a corner of the bookshelves at random, my hand passing over stout biographies and memoirs on autopilot. Why had that man been frowning at me? Perhaps I had been mistaken. In a small town, you were always bumping into the same people.

I sighed and tried to distract myself with some books. I wasn't sure what I wanted. Either in the bookshop, I supposed, or life in general. Christmas was over; there were no more presents to buy. When I spotted a cookbook by one of Vanessa's favourite chefs, I willed away thoughts of her upcoming birthday. I veered towards paperback fiction instead, my eyes scanning for any French authors on my to-read list. Next to one of the ladders a display of young-adult books caught my eye, dragons and roses swirling around the covers.

Next to the display, Mia was stacking some shelves. She looked the consummate bookseller, in a pair of stylish glasses, with her curly hair tied back.

I immediately felt guilty for not replying to her message from a few days ago. I should have remembered that St Rule was not like London: if you ghosted someone, there was a high chance they would come back to haunt you.

I murmured her name in the quiet shop. At first I wasn't sure she had heard me. Then she turned from the bottom shelf.

'Sorry I didn't get a chance to reply,' I continued. 'It's been non-stop with the family, you know.' Non-stop mince pies and Christmas TV.

'Yeah, of course,' she replied, steadying a tower of pristine hardbacks on either side. In this light, her olive skin looked paler than before, even anaemic. I pictured her in the school library at lunchtime, when I was on duty as a monitor. I would be the one sitting amid piles of books, while she studied at a table.

She looked around with an awkward smile, a few strands of hair stuck to her forehead. I realized it must be almost closing time and I should drive home for dinner. 'Great to see you the other night,' I said. I was about to turn and leave, when I felt an overwhelming impulse to ask something. I wasn't sure when I would get another chance. 'I was wondering. You sounded kinda *worried* about Joanie. Is everything OK? Have you seen her?'

Her face changed. 'No.' She stood up and took a step closer towards me. 'It's just one of those things I don't have a good feeling about.'

'What gives you that impression?' I didn't know what to make of this. She had been awful to Joanie. Adam had said she hated her.

'Have *you* seen her over the years?' Mia asked. 'I remember you were friends.'

'No . . . I mean we were friends, yes, but I haven't seen her since . . .' I couldn't bring myself to mention the party '. . . school ended. Same with you?'

'Oh, no. No. We worked together. That's the thing.' She was talking in a lowered voice, so the other customers wouldn't hear.

'What?' This was great news. 'Where?'

'At Hallowed Ground, by the Divinity Library. It's got a different name now.'

'For how long?'

She thought about it. 'About a month after school. Then I left.' She looked down at the carpet.

'OK, but Joanie stayed?'

'Yeah, she seemed to.' She looked up at me, biting her lip. 'This is what I wanted to talk to you about. But I have to lock up now.' She walked away to switch off a light at the back.

I didn't really want to leave the conversation, but when I looked at my watch, it had gone six o'clock. 'Sure thing,' I said, walking behind her, as she made her way down a few steps towards the front door. 'I guess I just wanted to know, why are you so concerned?' It came out wrong.

She looked round at me. 'Why am *I* so concerned? If you have a couple of minutes, I'll tell you.' She went over to put the keys in the door and turn off another light, a less-than-subtle signal to the stragglers, who left their seats to pay. I hovered around the Scottish section and started leafing through *The Big Book of Lochs*.

Once the last customer had gone, I watched Mia cash up at the antique counter. I had the feeling she had been waiting to get this off her chest, to set the record straight to one of her classmates. 'To be honest,' she said, 'the thing that Adam denied was that we *were* together. It was way before the *you know*.'

She meant the beach party. As she counted out

coins by the till, I noticed her nails were bitten down on her thin fingers. She seemed nervy. The kind of person who pulled all-nighters for her PhD, wired on caffeine, hands shaking. Maybe even someone who had the potential to be obsessive.

'Believe it or not, back then I thought he had broken up with Joanie. That's basically what he told me.' She looked up at me, annoyed at the memory. Their night in the dunes had been a funny story to tell among our year group for months and even years afterwards.

'He was a liar. I didn't really want to talk to him the other night, at Altman's. You know what I mean? I was actually hoping he wouldn't be there. I met him at one of the band nights. Everyone loved him, didn't they? God. We used to go to the cinema together, in Dundee, just as friends, really. He would pick me up in his car and take me to his house. His mother knew me. Then we just got really wasted at that party. It was partly because I knew he was going to leave. It was so embarrassing.'

I wanted to believe everything she said, but I was unsure. 'Did you not see Joanie at that party?' I said, as non-judgementally as possible. 'I suppose they were always pretty couple-y.' I could hear the defensiveness in my voice. They couldn't take their hands off each other. Maybe I still had some jealousy too, towards Adam.

'Look, I can't really remember. Everything felt so

dramatic back then. Life or death. I feel bad.' She picked up her backpack and stuffed a reusable water bottle inside it, then wound a rainbow-striped scarf round her neck. Was she being dramatic now too? 'Joanie gave as good as she got, but we were so young. I don't blame her for anything.'

I nodded, but it sounded a bit patronizing. I didn't know whether to stay or go.

'When she came to work at the café, she was *not* happy to see me. I think she was on a campaign to get me fired.'

'That was why you left?'

'God, no. It was the other people. One of the guys in particular. Bad vibes, to say the least.'

This conversation was moving at some pace and I was trying hard to catch up. I wanted to tell her about the Christmas cards. But could I trust she was telling the truth? I had buttoned my coat as I followed her to the exit.

'Do you need a lift home or anything? I've got the car,' I said. My breath was steaming in the chilly evening air.

'That's so kind,' she replied, her nose starting to go red as she looked up. 'I'm only a short walk away.'

'Walking?' I replied. 'It's dark. I'll give you a lift.'

Inside the car, it felt quieter and more intimate. The conversation slowed, even reversed into something more polite. 'Weird to be back here. Do you find the same?' asked Mia, as she looked out of the passenger window at the town's Christmas lights blurring past. 'It's so old and traditional, but at the same time, there are so many people, young people, coming and going. My flat's just down here.'

I nodded, taking a left turn at the steep hill outside the old town, lined with flats and pubs. 'Do you like being back?' I asked. She had told me how her parents had moved to Bristol while she was at Oxford.

'I do,' she said. 'Although it's a case of not being able to step into the same river twice. One of the first places I went, when I moved back here, was the café we used to work at. It's under new management. I searched for Joanie online, asked around. Like you, I didn't get anywhere. At least at first. There's this blog I'm going to send you. Another academic has looked into the guy I mentioned and he's not a good egg. This is my flat here.'

I was expecting something different. It was a beige, anonymous block on the edge of the suburbs.

'Joanie and I were pretty good friends at school,' I said. 'It's strange. You know, we tend to think that we can find anything online, but sometimes we can't. Tatey and Adam don't seem to know anything about her. If Cara knew, she would have told Tatey. Joanie's stepdad didn't want to talk about it. Graham doesn't know where she is and neither does his family, her old *neighbours*. You're the only person who has told me anything.'

'And I don't know where she is either,' said Mia. 'It's not through want of trying since I came back. I hadn't thought about her for years until I read that blog. I feel this sense of guilt.'

That was exactly how I felt too. Guilty. Like I had been a terrible friend. It felt as though by solving this one problem, all my others might go away.

'Is there something else?' Mia asked. 'You look like you're not telling me everything.' Nothing got past Mia. She had been watching me as closely as I had been watching her.

'Someone's been sending me these Christmas cards,' I said. 'They're notes really, telling me not to look for Joanie.'

I watched concern spread over Mia's face. We were sitting in the dark driveway outside her flat.

'I know. It's creepy. Whoever it is clearly knows who I am, where I live. Each one is just a few sentences, though.' If only I had brought the cards in my notebook with me today, I could have shown her.

'Have you gone to the police?' she asked.

'I feel like they won't believe me, or they'll think I'm making a fuss over nothing.' I had never said this out loud, but it was true. 'I remember at school once, Tatey got beaten up when we were walking home in fourth year. Like properly assaulted by these two bams in the year above. They cracked his head against a lamppost. He had a concussion. I can't even remember their names now, but I knew them back then. I knew *exactly* who they were. We told the police. We told them where the guys lived. And did they *do* anything? Did they fuck. I felt like a right . . . You know. Who's gonna be bothered about a couple of Christmas cards coming through my letterbox? I don't want to tell my parents either, 'cause it will worry them too much.'

'I see,' she said, thinking. 'I don't want to jump to conclusions, but I'll send you this blog and maybe we can talk about it again. Be prepared, though. It's quite intense.' She sighed. 'Well, I'd best be off. It's been good to see you. Let me know if you're in town tomorrow?'

'Oh? Why?' I asked.

'It's New Year's Eve, of course,' she said, with a smile. 'If you wait here for two secs, I want to lend you something.'

She ran into the building. A few minutes later, she came out and gave me a green clothbound volume, the size of a hymn book. 'This gives a bit more background,' she said. 'He lent it to me. I left before I could give it back. It's worth a read.'

I looked down at the title, printed in gold. *Plant and Ritual.*

Extract from 'Who's Afraid of the Dark?' by Joanie Sinclair, 2012

You never know how you might react in a situation like this. Flight, fight, freeze. Most people at school would say I'm quiet. When I saw that hand, I was loud. A scream flew out of my mouth like a banshee. Tinsel leaped off the bed and, with my eyes shut tight against the glare, I heard her bolt out the door. There was a clatter and stomp of feet. The deep, wordless shout of a man. Then the room was dark again and his footsteps thundered down the stairs.

29

Joanie, September 2013

It was only when they were at the petrol station that Joanie saw the clifftops in the distance, like the edge of the Earth. From inside David's small maroon car, the sea stretched out around them from three different angles. The petrol station was retro; it looked as though no one had come here since the eighties. All three of them stayed seated, with Joanie in the back, while the attendant filled the tank. He was a moustachioed man in overalls who smiled at her through the window.

'You've made a friend,' said Erin, from the passenger seat.

'Did you say it's a holiday let?' asked Joanie. She could hardly afford to pay her share of the petrol, let alone the accommodation. Erin had never brought it up, but it seemed obvious now.

'No,' said David, tapping the steering wheel in front of him anxiously, as if the man was taking too long. 'It's my family's, really. Sometimes we rent it out.' The man had stopped filling the tank and beckoned them to follow him into the shop to pay. David seemed barely to notice.

'Come on,' said Erin, stretching her petite limbs. She held out two fingers to the moustachioed man. *Two minutes.* 'It's yours, David. Tell her the truth.'

Erin had seemed on edge for the entire morning, while they drove the five hours up the coast from St Rule. Joanie had dragged herself out of bed at the crack of dawn, even before Elise had woken her mother and Gary. Erin and David had picked her up in the car while she was still half asleep.

It was only when Joanie had started seeing signs for Caithness, as the peatland grew flatter, that it dawned on her she didn't know exactly where they were staying. The cottage had been mentioned, but not an address. Her mother hadn't bothered to ask when Joanie had told her about the trip a few weeks ago. During the journey, Joanie had heard Erin refer to a place called Fulmar's Bluff. They had talked about Vik, who had volunteered to look after the café in their absence, and what a shame it was that he couldn't come. She sensed something disingenuous in David's tone. He was still funny about phones so Erin had asked her not to bring one. The whole point of going there, Erin had said, was to get away from technology and the modern world. She missed Vik, but she still wasn't sure what to think about him leaving in a few weeks. The change of scene would do her good.

'Is the cottage yours, David?' Joanie asked, keen to know more.

'OK, yeah, I suppose you're right,' said David, taking off his seatbelt and opening the car door to the windswept forecourt of the petrol station. There was an unusual note of sarcasm in his voice. 'It is my place. I bought it outright after my grandparents died.'

Erin turned in her seat and rubbed her fingers together. *Money.* Joanie smiled, but she could feel how uptight David was becoming. His exchanges with Erin had been terse. It was the first time she had seen any real tension between the couple. It reminded her of when she was little and her mother had argued with the partner before Gary.

'Wait,' Joanie said. 'Can I pay? I need to go to the bathroom.'

'I'm not letting you pay—' David began.

'Take this.' Erin passed her a credit card, her tanned arm stretching out between the two front seats. 'I insist.'

In the safety of the petrol-station toilet, Joanie took out her phone, which she had hidden in her fleece pocket. She wanted to unplug from modern life as much as the next person, but you never knew. A one-line email from Vik's university address was waiting for her. *Let me know when you arrive.* So he did care after all. She had last emailed him a couple of hours ago, when they had stopped in Strath Horne to stretch their legs.

Almost there, she replied. She was pleased to see there were still a few bars of signal. She realized he wouldn't get the message until after his shift. Perhaps he would close early for the weekend.

Quickly, she opened a map on her phone, to see where on earth they were. There it was, Fulmar's Bluff, a place on the cliffs a couple of miles down the road. The photos looked pretty, but bleak.

She couldn't resist checking social media, while she was there. It felt oddly reassuring. The first photo that popped up was of the old fountain on Martyr's Street, posted by none other than Cara.

Wait, was she there? In St Rule? How could she be? Joanie refreshed the page and the photo disappeared. Even though they had drifted apart in the past few weeks, how could Cara not have told her? She bit her lip. There were no further details. She had to get back to the car, or Erin would start to wonder.

'Alright, love?' The man in the overalls smiled at her as Joanie paid with the credit card. She looked briefly at the chocolate bars and crisps along the counter. They had bought provisions at a small supermarket in Thurso about half an hour ago so she couldn't justify a KitKat. Maybe on the way home.

When she got back into the car, David seemed in a better mood, excited even. They took the tree-lined main road downhill until it curved into a vast, desolate peatland, dotted with small tufts of grass. Joanie's previous experience of the Highlands had been full of craggy hills, forests and snow-topped mountains during her Duke of Edinburgh expedition, but this landscape was so *empty*. Long rectangles of farm buildings lay some distance to her right as they drove past. When she looked closer, she saw they were abandoned. A tractor rusting by a tumbledown cowshed, its roof pocked with holes.

There, she saw it: a grey cottage on the green clifftop. The sun was hidden behind cloud. Their only welcoming party was a host of rosebay willowherb, waving in the wind.

30

Cameron, 30 December 2023

Back at home, after dinner, I flicked through the old hardback book that Mia had lent me. A postcard, showing a dramatic Highland coastline, marked a chapter called 'The Witch's Plant'. I cast my eye over pages that described so-called 'witches' or wise women, from fifteenth-century Europe, who burnt henbane seeds to send them into a trance. Some mixed the plant with fat or oils into a 'flying ointment' that they rubbed all over their body. Medieval clergymen believed this helped the women to fly, either in their body or their mind.

The chapter mentioned a Benedictine monk who described a great multitude of women under the influence, seduced by demons, riding through the night on the backs of wild beasts. There was a Dominican theologian who recorded suspected witches whose usage of the ointment took them into deeply unconscious states.

Quite what this had to do with Joanie, I wasn't entirely sure. I picked up my phone and clicked on the link Mia had sent me. It was a basic white website called *No to Nightshade*. The first page read:

> If you are new to the blog, here are two things you should know.
>
> Henbane is a plant that grows in the UK. It is a hallucinogen, but it is also a poison. It is a member of the nightshade family. A dose can make you feel like you are flying. A larger dose will send you to sleep for ever.

Maybe this was how medieval witches got their kicks, but why was that relevant now?

> David Henderson, a Cambridge academic campaigning to change the legal status of henbane, is a dangerous man. He is amassing a legion of followers to lobby the government to legalize the use of henbane for 'medicinal purposes and research'.

I was starting to understand. I guessed this must be the 'tricky' person Mia had worked with. There was a menu with lots of different subject headings. I clicked on the one entitled 'David Henderson pt 1'. It read:

David Henderson is a predator. While he seems, at first sight, like an unassuming, charming man, this is all part of a carefully contrived image. Behind the academic façade lies an egomaniac. I first encountered him at one of his now infamous informal lectures, where he asks to recruit new, often younger people in his field, to help him with his 'research'. Do not fall for this. His research is illegal and taking part is seriously dangerous. He relies on the good faith of students.

I read on:

Obsessed with the powerful and illegal use of the drug henbane, he believes that the Vikings were on to something. That henbane is misunderstood. This belief, as you may or may not be aware, is gaining traction in certain corners of academia. We are beginning to see the therapeutic effects of LSD, mushrooms and even ketamine. I argue in a number of my blog posts why henbane is not another therapeutic drug like those mentioned above. It is only a poison.

I clicked through pages of quotes from scientific research, which seemed to be the author's background. It veered from academic paper to character assassination. One of the chapter headings caught my eye.

SOMETHING DARKER?

In 2013 a woman died on the cliffs of Fulmar's Bluff in Caithness. It was ruled a tragic fatal accident, but there is growing evidence that something darker was at play. The woman had been staying with David Henderson and a female friend at the time.

I froze. My mind went back to Joanie's house and Gary's hostility. Had he been reacting in pain? I remembered how on edge Mia had been. Was it too difficult to tell me out loud?

I searched online for *Fulmar's Bluff*.

Tripadvisor reviews and a satellite map. I zoomed in, looking at a lone cottage on a steep promontory. I magnified the map further, with a pang of self-consciousness as I squinted at the screen. Then, with horror, I turned back to the book, *Plant and Ritual*, and pulled out the postcard from its pages. The very same cliffs rose steeply out of the sea.

My mouth felt dry. This was too much to process. Did I want to search for more? I typed in *Fulmar's Bluff, fatal accident* and hit 'enter' before I could stop myself. A few articles came up, all with the same information.

A young woman has died after falling from the cliffs at Fulmar's Bluff in Caithness. It is understood that the woman was staying in the area with friends when she fell. One of her friends alerted the emergency services.

At roughly 9 a.m. this morning the Thurso RLNI lifeboat was called to the 200ft cliff top of Fulmar's Bluff, a small peninsula on Caithness's rugged northern coast when friends had discovered the woman missing.

The site is close to where, last year, a man slipped and broke his ankle. Locals say the area is notoriously dangerous.

I tried a few more search terms, trying and failing to find any more significant details. I wished I hadn't read this before bed. I wanted to see Mia again, if only to talk to her about it in person. Against my better judgement, I looked back at the latest blog entry, which was a link to a video, posted a few months ago.

HALLOWED GROUND: THE HENBANE CULT NO ONE WANTS YOU TO KNOW ABOUT

One of those now ubiquitous automated voices was talking in rapid hyperbole while stock footage of cult gatherings and psychedelic drugs bombarded the screen by way of an introduction. I could barely keep up. The video cut to a photo of Cambridge University, then one of Dr Henderson, now a member of the Department of Anglo-Saxon, Norse and Celtic, then to a fuzzy hidden camera. We were in a large, crowded room, listening to someone speaking off camera. There was more grainy footage of people lying in a dim room on the floor, at a retreat, droning music playing. I peered closely at the screen. Maybe Joanie was among them. Part of me hoped she was.

More subtitles over a video told me that the filmmaker was being offered a drink 'spiked with henbane'. I watched a hand hold it up close to the camera. Then the screen went black.

The voiceover came back, with a freeze-frame. 'STAY TUNED FOR MORE.' I clicked around on the filmmaker's profile, but no more videos had been uploaded.

Mia, I messaged, *what the hell's going on?*

Extract from 'Who's Afraid of the Dark?' by Joanie Sinclair, 2012

I lay still in bed, long after I had heard the front door slam shut and Tinsel had returned to my feet. I called the police, who came and interviewed me in the middle of the night. I told them everything I have recounted here. I tried calling and texting my mum, but she was fast asleep.

The police said I was too young to be left home alone. I said I was fifteen. They said, 'Exactly.' They made me call my dad. He finally picked up the phone, confused and bleary from his house in Glasgow. 'I'm coming, babe,' he said. It would take a couple of hours. The police made sure the house was secure. I felt so lucky. So unlucky, of course, and yet lucky to have survived. It could have been so much worse.

31

Joanie, September 2013

The interior of the cottage wasn't as photogenic as Joanie had been hoping. It reminded her of the bothy they had stayed in at school, with faded gingham curtains and a pine-clad kitchen, a throwback from the eighties. David clearly hadn't made any updates since his grandparents had owned it.

She took out a few items from her backpack in the small room with twin beds, covered with chintzy duvets. Erin and David had the double next door. The two bedrooms were on the ground floor, along with the kitchen-diner and a small, stark living room with brown furniture. In spite of the décor, it felt good to have this space to herself. She stopped unpacking and lay on the bed by the window, closing her eyes to the rush of the waves nearby. The sea sounded as though it was on the other side of the wall – the cliffs were that close. This was the holiday she needed, a small escape. A blank slate. The sun had come out and the view from her bedroom window was gorgeous and clear. You could even see the lighthouse a little way down the coastline. Further out, towering sea stacks rose from the water like old teeth.

She sat up and looked at her phone. No word from Vik. The trip would have been so much better if he had come along. She still wasn't sure if it really *was* David he didn't want to spend time with, or her. She took a photo of the view. If she posted it, no one would know but her school friends, the people who had been documenting evidence of their travels every day since exams had ended. She wanted them to know that she was also somewhere beautiful and mysterious. Her life hadn't ended just because Adam had left her behind. The screen went grey. Her photo wouldn't load. She tried again, but there was no signal.

Erin called from the kitchen. Joanie tried uploading the photo one last time without any luck. She was sure that, somewhere around here, there would be signal. She thought clifftops were good for that kind of thing.

When she went into the kitchen, it was empty. She opened the back door and inhaled the salty air. She saw Erin and David standing at the end of the garden that swept down to the cliff edge, cups of tea in their hands. They seemed to be getting on better than they had on the car journey. As she walked up to them, she felt a strange pang of disappointment that they hadn't made tea for her. David was pointing at something along the rocky coast.

'The raiders would have come from this direction,' he said. He turned to look at Joanie. 'See that mound over there, with the stones? That used to be a medieval settlement. I'm going to walk over and take some photos of it later, if either of you wants to come.'

Erin shook her head. She opened her mouth, as though about to speak, then decided against it.

'What?' David asked. 'Go on. Say what's on your mind. You've clearly wanted to all day.'

Erin sighed. 'I was just thinking of what you were telling me about this raid,' she replied. 'I mean, does the violence ever get too much for you?'

Joanie held her breath. She almost wanted to laugh at the hostility.

'What?' asked David, squinting at her in the sun, challenging her to say more.

'Like, these were *real* attacks. Do you ever think about that? People were murdered. Monks. Women and children. You keep going over and over these violent *massacres*, like they're, I don't know . . . a means to an end.' Erin was breathless as she spoke.

'Do I ever *think* about them? It's not like I'm writing a *book* on the subject.' David shook his head and started walking away. 'Something's up with you. I'm not engaging with this.'

Joanie wanted to go back to her bedroom, but

she didn't want to follow David into the house. She hoped she wouldn't become a third wheel this weekend, an awkward bystander to whatever was going on between them.

'Come on,' said Erin. 'Let's get some space.'

They picked their way over the next field in silence, walking in the opposite direction from the settlement.

'That place gives me the creeps,' Erin said. 'It was the scene of brutal violence. David is obsessed with that.'

'He's writing his book on it?' Joanie asked, as they sat cross-legged under a lone, twisted tree in the field. She could see distant white specks of sheep behind them.

'On Maeyar. *Aiden and the Berserkers of Maeyar*, he says it's going to be called.'

'Sounds like a band name,' Joanie said, thinking of some of the groups that came through Adam's Neuklear Fusion. 'I think Aiden came up on the Maeyar island tour. We definitely had a few books about him.'

'David's looking at things from a very different angle,' Erin replied, then changed the subject. 'My field of research is medieval botany, essentially. I've always loved plants. I want to bring them further into my meditation practice or maybe set up a separate workshop. For example, I'm researching how people in the Middle Ages would scatter or strew herbs like apple mint, sage and thyme in their houses to make them fragrant and ward off creepy-crawlies. I'm thinking of trying it here. Maybe we could pick some tomorrow. They're all growing in the garden. Sweet maudlin too, which they used to repel ticks.'

'Sweet maudlin? Let's hope we don't have to try that one out,' said Joanie, checking her bare ankles. She thought for a minute. 'What's your favourite herb?'

'I like sage. I could talk about its medicinal properties for hours. The Anglo-Saxons used to say, "Why should man die when he has sage?"' She paused. 'It was seen as a cure-all. I like henbane too. It's so misunderstood. What David's doing with his research is so interesting. I'll be the first to admit that. It's the violent massacres I don't like.'

'Henbane,' said Joanie. 'I remember from David's talk. The berserkers.'

'Yeah, but it's not like that with the right amount. I've tried it multiple times, and it's perfectly safe if you know what you're doing. It really chills you out.'

Erin was looking at Joanie, her hair glowing in the sunlight, as if she was about to suggest that they try it. Instead, she began to pick daisies in the grass around them and thread them into a garland. Her fingers moved nervously, like she was thumbing a rosary.

'Is everything OK between you and David?' Joanie asked.

Erin looked down at the flowers, seeming not to hear her at first. 'It's complicated,' she said. 'All this research he's doing. He's been given this grant and everything. It's like a *hundred* thousand. I like his ideas, but he's not . . .' She stopped herself. 'I'd prefer not to talk about it. He's about to hit the big time and he knows it. Everyone in that department – everyone in his *field* – thinks he's, like, so incredible for working on this fucking manuscript. Well, little do they know . . .' She stopped herself. 'Anyway, I'm here to relax. I hope you can too.'

Joanie nodded and started picking the daisies by her feet. Then they closed their eyes and sat listening to the waves, breathing steadily in and out, while time slipped away.

'Aiden of Maeyar was an amazing man,' said David, as they ate a bean stew at the small, candlelit table in the kitchen-diner. It was still fairly light outside, but David had drawn the gingham curtains. The wind had picked up and the waves had started to smash against the steep cliffs. 'He learned so much about mind expansion through henbane and other plants, things that had only been known in the Norse world. You can tell, especially in these testimonies, that his whole life changed through his experiments. He describes the revelation as a "clear, beautiful light descending. The light of the natural world."'

They ate for a few moments in silence, before David began speaking again. 'When I translate his words, it's like he's speaking through me. It's an incredible feeling, really. Almost holy. He writes about the future, a future he sees after one night taking a kind of henbane tea. That there will be a man who will unlock secrets.'

Erin looked down at her food. Joanie could feel David looking at her, as she did the same. She wanted her to say something to that, but she couldn't find the words. He had a look in his eyes that reminded her of the elderly woman who ran the Jesus Bus and handed out the evangelical comics. Holy Hannah.

'Do you ever go back to the States?' Joanie asked Erin, hoping that a change of subject would pierce the tense atmosphere.

'Oh, no, not really,' Erin replied. 'My parents aren't close. They don't want to know what I'm doing. They didn't approve of me being with David, quite frankly. It was stressful for a while, wasn't it?' she said, a little tersely, looking at David. 'They're pretty religious, among other things. But now I'm used to it. We both are.'

Joanie didn't believe her and she didn't know what was so offensive about David, really. Eccentric perhaps, confident, but that was all.

Once they had finished their bowls of stew, David and Erin exchanged a glance, then Erin walked through the room, blowing out the candles, while

David switched on the droning sounds they used for meditation. The room sank into darkness and Joanie's heart began to beat faster. She didn't like it. Erin knew she had panic attacks and that the pitch dark reminded her too much of the break-in, the night she had been alone in the house. She dug her nails into her hands.

'Have you heard of exposure therapy?' Erin's voice from somewhere in the room. 'I think this could help your anxiety in a major way.' Joanie balked at her directness.

'It's just the dark, Joanie,' said David, from another point in the room. 'There's nothing to be afraid of.'

Had this been planned in advance? 'Can I get some fresh air?' Joanie asked.

She stumbled out into the garden, past tall fox-gloves and rosebay willowherb, then down the slope of lawn in the grey dusk, dipping down out of sight. By the back gate, she took out her phone. There was still very little signal. She could see specks of light from a ship on the horizon and houses further down the coast. She looked back at the cottage, then walked to the edge of the cliff, by the railing. The drop below was alarmingly sheer. She received a notification to say her earlier photo had been posted. The signal was working. An email reply popped up from Vik. As she opened it, the phone lit up her face. *Your friend came by the café. I think she was trying to surprise you.*

Cara. She wanted more than ever to talk to her. The wind was getting stronger, pushing at her back. Joanie started to reply – but someone shoved her hand, hard, and her phone went flying into the grey-dark.

She made out David's face, coming close. 'What the fuck?' he hissed. 'No phones. That was the condition of coming to my house.' His eyes were wild with fury. 'You knew that.'

Joanie pushed him angrily out the way and tried to look for the phone in the long grass. David kicked something that went skidding under the fence, towards the the cliffs. She heard a skitter of stones.

'What did you just do? Was that my phone?' She was incensed.

'You're here to help with my research. You're here to help Erin,' he replied, his voice hot with anger. 'After *everything* we've done for you.'

Joanie bolted back up the garden in long strides, her face burning. David ran and caught her up. 'Drink this,' he said, holding up an open flask and pushing it against her mouth. 'Drink it. It's what we came here to do.' His tone was sarcastic.

'What?' Joanie spluttered, as something bitter splashed over her lips and into her mouth. She started to choke, till her eyes were watering. 'Get away from me!' she screeched, turning and running to the back door of the cottage. When she looked back, he was still standing in the garden, facing the sea. She could see his broad shoulders rise and fall.

She entered the dark kitchen-diner, where the music was still playing. She almost fell over Erin, who was lying, eyes closed, on a mat on the floor.

'Are you OK?' Joanie whispered.

'I'm waiting,' Erin murmured 'for it to take hold.' Joanie looked around the silent house.

'The tea?' Joanie asked, cautiously. 'How long does it take?'

'Oh, a few hours. I like to meditate.'

'David just tried to make me drink something.' Joanie said breathlessly. 'I think it was the same . . . the henbane.'

'Yes,' Erin drawled. 'He likes to help people experiment. For his research.' Her silky hair lay loose around her shoulders.

Joanie glanced towards the window. No sign of David. 'It wasn't like that. I think I drank some.'

'Don't worry. He knows what he's doing, when he prepares it. He grows it here. It's a plant that likes sandy soil. Butterflies and bees like the nectar.' Erin was rambling. 'Anyway, people used to take it for toothache.'

Joanie knelt down beside her, touching her arm. 'No, Erin. He's angry with me.'

Erin opened her eyes and said calmly, 'Well, I'm angry with him.'

'What?'

BLUFF

'He thinks I don't know what he's been up to. After *all* the support I've given him. Believe me. People think he's a genius, finding this manuscript. The lines he quotes! Well, I know now he's a fraud.'

32

Cameron, 31 December 2023

My mother kept looking at me with some concern as we drove to the supermarket to pick up food for their New Year's Eve drinks.

'Yes, Mum?' I asked, hearing an edge to my voice.

She kept her eyes on the road. 'I didn't say anything! You haven't let me know what you want for tonight. I invited Stuart and his family, but they said they were having their own thing. He said he'd told you about it?'

'I don't know that I can go, actually,' I replied, ignoring the last bit.

We parked the car in silence. We weren't the chattiest family, but I could tell something was up. I had only come along for the ride. I had noticed my mother was finding it harder to lift heavy shopping out of the car, so I wanted to give her a hand, as well as making sure I found the right ingredients for the roast pork dish I had promised to make tomorrow, New Year's Day. I hadn't made it before. The recipes

I knew back to front reminded me of Valentine's Days and birthdays I'd rather forget. Birthdays. Shit.

The supermarket was so busy with people buying last-minute booze and supplies for the next couple of days that I wished we had planned ahead. I grabbed a few discounted Christmas treats, but I couldn't look at another mince pie until next December.

I remembered I needed to stay on task with finding the ingredients for my recipe, while also keeping an eye on my mother, who was darting in and out of shoppers, piling the trolley with God knew what. We already had enough food in the cupboards to survive nuclear disaster.

Just then, I saw her stop short at the card aisle. She looked around for me, then beckoned me over. I realized she had led us there on purpose. 'You did buy a card, didn't you?' she asked.

'Sorry?' I knew where this was going. The realization hit me with a slow dread. 'Oh, Vanessa's birthday? Yeah, I remembered. Sorted.' This was so unlike me, scrambling to cover my arse. It never felt like the right time. Her birthday was in two days' time. London was a million miles away. What would be going on down there in a couple of days? Balloons in a cocktail bar most likely. Sympathetic female friends. I could picture them now. Olivia, Priya, Marta, Jess. They would make a fuss of her. And anyway . . .

'Our present should arrive just in time,' my mother said. 'I sent it to her parents' house.'

'No! What?' I couldn't keep the alarm from my voice as I fumbled with my phone to try and warn Vanessa.

'No? What's going on, Cameron?'

Nothing good ever came from those words. 'Why don't you tell me?' I asked. My face was growing hot. I looked around me. The aisle was busy. I could bump into someone I knew at any second.

'It's just a small gift . . .' She squinted at me from behind her large glasses, shopping basket in hand.

I didn't hear what she said next. Rows of discounted Christmas cards stood in front of me. Towards the bottom there was a small multipack, with the same design that had been pushed through my letterbox. The rabbit in the snowy field, the cottage against the night sky.

'What's up, Cameron?' my mother asked.

I was already striding towards the checkout.

'You could at least have *told* me you were going to the car,' my mum said, when she joined me, clearly displeased, as I lifted the last of the shopping bags into the boot. 'Always so dramatic. What's happened?'

'I'm not dramatic,' I said, thumping the boot lid down and shoving the empty trolley across towards the others that snaked along the store front.

'*Cameron*,' my mum hissed, making me feel like I was sixteen and drunk.

I got into the car and yanked on my seatbelt. I was going to say it. Then she would leave me alone.

My mum slammed her door. This was not a good start. On the other side of the windscreen, the sky was threatening to rain.

'We broke up. OK?' I wanted out of here. This wasn't fair.

She looked at me, her expression changing to sympathy.

My voice dropped to a mutter. 'We're not getting married.'

My mother nodded calmly. 'And when did this happen, Cameron? You should have said something.'

'It doesn't matter when it happened. I don't want to talk about it.'

'OK. I'm just trying to understand. So this is maybe why you've come home.'

Maybe nothing. 'I can't give you a reason, OK, Mum? If I could, I would!' An empty void stretched out before me. Then I felt a pang of rage. 'While we're on the subject of relationships, anything going on that I should know about with you and Stuart?' Skulking about the garden, inviting my mother to his stupid party. Something was up. Maybe he was even the letter writer. Maybe they had been getting it on in the garden shed. It was too much to bear.

'Cameron, no. *No!* Don't be ridiculous. We're just

friends, that's all. Gosh, you have a wild imagination. You always did. We both like gardening and doing the crossword and . . .' Already her tone was giving her away.

'*Mum*. Look at you, you're practically blushing.'

'Is it so bad?' she said. 'To have a friend? I get lonely, you know, sometimes.'

I spluttered. 'Not too lonely, I hope. What does Dad think of all this?'

'Oh, for goodness' sake, come off it. "All this"? You're being ridiculous. What do you take me for? You're my son. You're meant to trust me.'

I didn't know what to say, so I sat in silence in the parked car. A blur of assignations ran through my head at top speed. Secret meetings in one another's cars after work. Dinner reservations far from home. Hotel rooms. These images, these memories, they weren't between my mum and Stuart. They were things I had done with a colleague at work. Another teacher.

My mum started the car engine. God knew what must have been going through her head.

My fiancée Vanessa wasn't stupid. Eventually, she had become suspicious about the number of times a fictitious friend called Brian had been texting me or that my department head had called me out of hours. One evening Brian's name had flashed up again and again when I had left my phone in our bedroom to take a shower. I had told Naomi, the colleague I was seeing, to be careful, but by that point we were in too deep, now I looked back. I had thought Naomi was someone significant in my life. She wasn't. She was just a hot English teacher. Maybe I had been scared of getting married. Maybe I had thought Vanessa and I weren't right for each other and didn't know what to do about it. Maybe I had simply liked the attention. Whatever I had been thinking, it had happened. And I had lost a woman who had cared about me. The sex with Naomi hadn't even been that good. But I refused to cry about it. It was my fault.

My mother did what she always did in awkward situations and put on the radio. The silence was filled by one of those polished, inauthentic voices of an easy-listening station. An eighties track started playing, its title on the tip of my tongue.

I looked out of the passenger window and fought back tears. I was pathetic.

Extract from 'Who's Afraid of the Dark?' by Joanie Sinclair, 2012

I tried to sleep in the car, as my dad drove, but I couldn't. I was still awake when the sun started to rise on the motorway. We stopped at a service station for petrol and bacon rolls. I was still awake when my mum's number buzzed on my phone. I could hardly tell her what had happened, because my dad was shouting so loud.

33

Joanie, September 2013

Joanie lay wide awake in her dark twin bed, tense with fear, thinking of her friend lying in the living room. She wanted to turn on the light, but for the first time in her life she felt safer this way. After an hour or so, she heard a door slam and raised voices. She strained to listen.

'Don't you dare touch me!' It was Erin, high-pitched and wild.

The drone of music stopped. There was another crash, the sound of something clattering to the floor.

'Don't look at me like that. I know everything!' Erin was yelling. 'I know how much you've lied. You're losing touch with reality. You are! You're not translating that thing. It's made up! You're making all that stuff up. You don't deserve that money, David.'

'For the love of God. What are you talking about?' That was David's voice, confident and calm, but belittling.

'I've started reading it myself. Your *translation*. It's not real. Aiden's predictions of the future? Bullshit.'

'Ah, for one thing, you can't *possibly* have read it. You have *no* idea what you're talking about. I've told you before. The words I translate are sacred. *Sacred*. He is speaking through me. Through my work.'

There was a deadly silence until Erin spoke again, quiet, reasoning. 'You're aware of how, um, *insane* you sound?'

'Then why are you the only one who doubts me, Erin? This is *years* of knowledge and research. It's even more than that. I don't know what I can say to convince you. I'm probably the most rational person you've ever known.'

'David.'

'You'd better have a long, hard think about what you're saying.'

Erin muttered something inaudible.

'I know she's in the next room. I gave her some too. Clearly, I didn't give you enough.'

'*David*, no.'

There was a clatter.

'David, get away from me. No. I don't *want* any more.'

A scraping of furniture, then another excruciating silence. Joanie tried to get up, but her body stayed frozen in the black of the bedroom. She tried again, but she couldn't move. She began to feel sick, a headache pinching at her temples. Back in the garden, when David had shoved the open flask in her face, she had swallowed some of the liquid.

As she tried to listen to more, the words became muffled and her eyes became heavy. She lost track of time, her brain drifting on the edge of consciousness, between reality and dream. Gradually, the dark walls became those of her teenage bedroom. Then they were the stone of a monastery. She looked down and the earth was far beneath her bare feet. She was outside, she was sure of it, looking down from a great height. She could see the patchwork of dark fields, trees and the ocean, with the tiny lights of boats floating on its surface like stars. Then, like a witch, she was flying through the night sky.

34

Cameron, New Year's Eve 2023

After the scene in the car with my mum, there was no way I was hanging around for New Year's Eve drinks with my parents and their small group of friends. I left just after they switched on the BBC's *Hogmanay Live*, to play in the background, with its folk bands and studio crowd and the lights of Princes Street. The show wasn't the same without Jackie Bird.

Tatey had said he would meet me at a new bar, the Auld Bothy, that had opened in St Rule on Martyr's Street. The inside was modelled on something between a gastro pub and a hay barn. The place started filling with students, back from the Christmas holidays down south with Ma and Pa. You could hear them a mile off. They looked so young and self-assured. It was funny; I would often find myself thinking about St Rule and my schooldays, but I barely remembered university in Glasgow. Maybe it was because I was a secondary-school teacher now and had to think about it every day. Granted, the London boys I taught were very different from my group of pals over a decade ago in our scruffy black uniforms. When I started my current job, I marvelled at the pupils' ironed shirts and clean, combed hair. I could imagine some of them coming to this very bar in a few years' time.

'Hey, man!' Tatey waved as he came to sit beside me at the table. He was looking surprisingly well-groomed. As we chatted, I realized how little I knew about him, given how much time we had spent together. I had no idea, for example, what he did for work.

'Stage technician,' he said, when I asked him. 'I thought you knew. Lighting, set building. Pyrotechnics occasionally.' He grinned at me. 'Local theatres, a few football matches, concerts, that kinda thing.' I remembered him helping Adam with the equipment for band nights. That van had come a long way.

Inside my jacket pocket was the book, *Plant and Ritual*, that I was planning to return. 'Mia might be along later,' I said. I had taken up her offer of a drink. The blog and its revelations had floored me, though. I remained more confused than ever.

'Oh, aye?' Tatey asked. He didn't seem pleased about Mia.

'Yeah. I bumped into her yesterday. She's actually really nice.'

He nodded disapprovingly. Then he pointed to the stage, by the bar, where a ceilidh band was scheduled to play. 'I don't like the way they've rigged that.'

'I'm sure they know what they're doing,' I said. 'It's interesting. Mia's also tried to find out what happened to Joanie.' The news story flashed back to my mind and, just as quickly, I pushed it away.

'Have you got those cameras set up on your house yet?'

'Nah.' No more Christmas cards had arrived, but I had actually raised the idea of getting a security system with my dad. He had laughed at me, saying I had spent too long in London. Nothing like that was needed in Monypenny. I would figure out something, I knew I would, but part of me hoped the letters had stopped for good. I was leaving the day after tomorrow anyway. I just wanted to make sure my parents didn't get any nasty surprises.

Four musicians walked on to the stage and started tuning their instruments. The bar had filled since we had first sat down, under the string of bare bulbs and bunting that adorned the timbered ceiling.

'Isn't it weird how no one knows where Joanie is, though?' I asked him. 'Even her stepdad couldn't tell me. Not that he doesn't know but . . .'

'Hang on, you're telling me you actually – what – doorstepped her family?' Tatey asked, aghast. 'Maybe just take it easy with that. You never know, eh? Something could be going on with the family.'

'Like what?' I asked. That had sounded like quite an informed opinion.

'I don't know. That's the exact point I'm making,' he replied.

'Alright, calm the ham,' I muttered, talking like I was at school again.

Tatey snorted and took a mouthful of his beer.

I fixed my eyes firmly on the band. The accordion player was wearing a tweed bunnet and a waistcoat. They looked like they might be shite. These students wouldn't know the difference. Just something to post on social media.

We stayed silent and stormy-faced as the group started with a jaunty folk song. It wasn't as bad as I had feared. Maybe this would make us feel better.

Tatey looked around the room, then spoke aggressively in my ear. 'I'm gonna be honest. I think you need to move on a bit. I don't know what you're hoping to find. We don't know where Joanie is. She was our friend back at school, so that's sad, that's awful sad, but you have a great life, you're gonna get married. I'm sure she's fine. Just put it behind you.'

I felt my jaw tense. I didn't need a motivational speech from Tatey of all people. 'OK . . .' I started awkwardly. 'If we're gonna be honest, mate, I feel like you're not exactly being straight with me.'

'What?' he asked, over the noise of the folk band. Everyone but us had started having a whale of a time.

I pretended I couldn't hear him and picked up the flyer that lay on the table. Scooby Dhu, the band was called. Of course it was. I looked around the room at the different faces, mostly younger, wondering if I might spot the guy I had seen on the beach. Had he really been following me? Or was it just a coincidence? There weren't many places to go in this small town.

'Cameron, why?' Tatey asked again in my ear, with a grab of my shoulder.

I shrugged him off. This was rubbish. Tatey had been a good, solid friend and I needed one of those right now. And yet. 'You know something,' I said. 'I know you know something and you're not telling me.'

Tatey knocked back his drink and looked me in the eye. 'You don't know what you're doing. Some things are better left alone. OK? Chill the *fuck* out.' Those were the strongest words I had ever heard from him. 'Anyway,' he continued, 'do you ever even think about *your* behaviour? What *you* did to her?'

'What I did to her? What did I do to her?'

'You know,' he said. 'School.' He put his glass down on the table and, with that, I watched him walk out into the final night of the year. Tatey was talking nonsense. He wasn't telling the truth. I had seen him play pranks over and over again. He could hide things. He could keep a poker face. I sat there in a daze as preppy twenty-somethings started making their way to the dance-floor, while the band played a cover of 'In A Big Country'. Probably the first time they had heard it. I had no idea what I was going to do with my life. As people rushed past me, laughing and singing along, I could feel myself drifting further into a state of mental isolation.

I sat there, nursing a pint, people-watching, until two delicate hands squeezed my shoulders. Finally, there she was.

Mia leaned over my shoulder, grinning like a pixie. She looked different without her glasses. She dragged me to my feet, without a word, and pushed me to the dance-floor. It was Hogmanay. I had now drunk enough to think I was a good dancer. A fresh year lay ahead of me. Think positive. I could make things work. It seemed clear now, as I danced, that London wasn't for me any more. It had served its purpose. As I looked into Mia's face, I felt happy. I twirled her tightly around the dance-floor. Her dark curls fell over her face and her eyes sparkled. There was barely room to move. We kept knocking into people, but that didn't bother me. We became breathless with laughter. I knew there were things I wanted to ask her, badly, but I didn't want to break the spell.

Finally, we went outside, pink-cheeked, for air. People had started to gather further down by the fountain, for the Bells. My eyes watered in the bitter cold.

'I read that blog,' I said, still a little out of breath, as we leaned against the wall of the stone-flagged entrance to the bar. There were artfully placed crates filled with plants at our feet and wooden shelves decorated with terracotta pots, like the outside of an expensive shed.

'What it describes is the reason I left,' she replied. 'I know it sounds mad. I started to work at Hallowed Ground. I needed some money and heard about the job through my dad's friends at the university. I got on OK with the manager, Erin. Then she wanted me to hang out more and more with her and David Henderson, whom she was in a relationship with, it turned out. He wanted me to help him with his research and planned these meet-ups, even when I was still at school, with me and some undergraduates in his department. We were told not to mention it. At first it was just academic stuff. Photocopying some journal articles, proof-reading an index. Sometimes we had dinner at his house. I have to admit, he made me feel quite special. One day, when school had finished, just after Joanie started, we all went to the Isle of Maeyar. I thought he was going to ask us to do mushrooms, in the name of research. I had heard him talk about it. But this was something else, the drug they talk about on the website, henbane. It's a hallucinogen, basically a poison. The book I gave you goes into more detail.'

'Yeah.' I said emphatically. 'I read it.' I handed her back *Plant and Ritual* from my jacket pocket.

'Well, he was really persistent, in this persuasive manner he has, and in the end . . . I tried it. Not too much, but enough.'

'Oh, God,' I said. 'Was Joanie there too?'

'No, she wasn't,' Mia replied, a little dismissively. 'She wasn't invited. It was one of the most awful experiences of my life. I felt like I was going to die. He remained sober, of course. It was just the students who started hallucinating. He had people who loved him, though, in academic circles. I think that was how he got away with it, somehow. Or they were too intimidated to make a fuss. Scared they would be blamed or get into trouble. Maybe they even believed in what he was doing. It looks like that's still happening, even worse.'

I let the gravity of her words sink in, as I watched more revellers walk past us. 'I'm so sorry that happened to you,' I said.

'I try not to think about it, most of the time. But I think that, subconsciously, coming back here was a way to try to face up to the past,' Mia replied softly. She shook her head. 'I didn't tell my parents about it at the time. I just left my job at that café. I mean, I had a place at Oxford. I wanted to get on with my life.'

From inside the bar, a countdown had started, people were shouting in unison: '*SIX . . . FIVE . . . FOUR . . .*'

I spoke as gently as I could against the racket. 'But you think that a similar thing happened to Joanie and that maybe . . .? I found some news articles. About the accident. A young woman in Caithness.'

'It's not looking good, is it?' she said, with a defeated smile, shivering in her party dress. 'I've been trying to find out more.'

I felt an urge to protect her. She was standing so close to me. I started to take off my jacket, to slip over her shoulders.

At that moment, the sky exploded loudly into fireworks, glittering silver and gold. Whooping and cheering rose from the fountain and the Auld Bothy. Every pub and home in town would be going crazy.

'Happy New Year,' I said, my head cocked to one side, opening my arms to hug her.

'Happy New Year,' she said, and threw her arms around my neck, to pull me in for a kiss. It was a brief, beautiful thing, like a shooting star. I couldn't stop looking at her. She had the most unbelievable eyes. I pushed a strand of her soft, dark hair away from her face. She leaned in close and breathed something into my neck. *Gotta go*. Then she started pacing backwards up the street.

'I promised my friend I'd go to her house party. Wanna come?' she asked, sounding like she genuinely wanted me to join her.

'I don't want to intrude.' It suddenly felt too much. After spending years with Vanessa, then the disastrous whirlwind that was Naomi, this was enough. I would savour the moment.

'Are you sure?' she asked, smiling. I liked how open she was. In London, everything was about hiding your real feelings for fear of seeming too keen.

'I'm sure,' I replied. Besides, I might feel old at a student house party, postgraduates or not. 'Keep the jacket, though. I'm serious.'

She looked thrilled, pulling it further around her shoulders. 'Really? I'll find you before you leave.'

With that, we raised our hands goodbye and I turned back towards the taxi rank. I was heading back to London so soon that it would be nice to catch my parents before they went to bed. Hopefully they had avoided Stuart's.

'Wait, Cameron!'

I turned round to see Mia running up to me. 'You left something in your pocket.'

Instinctively, I tapped my jeans, to check I had my phone and wallet.

'Here.' She thrust something into my hand, gave me a quick peck on the cheek and ran off down the street again, her hair bouncing on her shoulders.

A white envelope. My heart sank. I had come to recognize the small square shape, the scrawl of the handwriting. Sure enough, it was a Christmas card, identical to the other two. The rabbit, the snowy field, the cottage, the night sky. Four things I never wanted to see again as long as I lived. Maybe it was time to tell the police after all.

I looked around me, impotently, knowing that realistically, whoever it was wouldn't be standing in the street. I pushed my way back into the bar, but saw no one I knew. There were so many students. A couple looked young enough to be my pupils. The bar was so crowded this evening it could have happened an hour ago. I had been so frustrated with Tatey that I had taken my eye off the ball. How could I have missed this?

The message inside sent a shiver down my spine: *It seems there is only one way for you to understand. Meet me at South Sands. Tomorrow. 2 p.m.*

Extract from 'Who's Afraid of the Dark?' by Joanie Sinclair, 2012

I often remember how I felt that night, like I felt I was going to die. I always wonder what the man must have wanted. Nothing had been taken from our house. The police dusted for fingerprints, but they never found him. It taught me something. That I can be brave. That I can stand up to people and use my voice. The fact I felt like I wanted to die has made me want to live. I want to see what the world has to offer.

35

Joanie, September 2013

The next morning was Sunday. Joanie found herself in the single bed, pulling up the duvet to block out the chill. Dark, aerial visions came back to her from the night before. Erin was asleep in the twin bed next to her. Joanie peered over. Something about her didn't look right. She had one arm over her face. Her hand was a horrible colour. A mannequin's hand. Joanie slid out of bed and touched it. Cold skin. The room became soundless, like the shock of diving under water. She moved Erin's arm away from her face. It was stiff. Her lips were pale and twisted, her eyes, open. Her chest was still, no breath.

Joanie fell to the floor. A violent retching sound came out of her mouth. Instinctively, she pushed a chair up against the door with a loud scraping sound. As she grasped her bed, like a drowning person with driftwood, a fist pounded the door.

'Joanie, you in there?' a voice growled. David.

Joanie froze.

'What was that noise?' he said. 'Come out. Come out now. Don't be silly.'

Joanie made herself small, like a child, hugging her knees. Her body was reacting while her mind was paralysed. She looked up to the window. Could she climb out of it? The thought ebbed, then flowed away.

'Joanie, there's nothing to be scared of. It's just me. You need to come out.'

Why? Her mind refused to think any further. She looked instead at the pink and blue roses that adorned the bedclothes.

'*Joanie*, I'm not leaving until you come out.'

She stood up and pulled away the chair, opening the door mechanically, as if her mother was on the other side.

A man's hand slapped her across the face. 'What the fuck did you do?' David asked, calm and collected. It was almost as though he hadn't moved a muscle.

Joanie touched her face. Her skin was burning. The hand was right there in front of her, alive. David leaned in, his breath in her ear. 'You did it,' he said. 'Didn't you? It's your fault.'

Clarity dawned, for a brief moment. 'We need to call the police,' Joanie said. Her phone. He had kicked it away.

'Don't incriminate yourself,' David said, as if scolding a child. 'You did it.'

His tone was strange. She looked at him in confusion. 'I did what?' Her heart was pounding. She couldn't articulate what she had seen in the bedroom. She thought of her phone, most likely broken at the bottom of the cliff. David's fault. 'You need to call the police,' she said evenly. 'On your phone.'

David was shaking his head. 'No, no. There is no phone. You've done a terrible thing. We need to get this straight.'

She looked over her shoulder and saw his bags packed in the hall.

'We're leaving,' he said. 'Fetch your stuff and get in the car.'

'*No*,' said Joanie. She stayed rooted to the spot. 'I'm not going in there. Her hands are cold.' Somewhere in Joanie's brain, a tiny bell was ringing.

'You want me to go to the police and tell them what you've done?' David asked. This was threatening behaviour, Joanie said to herself, as if trying to make sense of things. He was not a good person. She tried to remember what had happened the night before, but shock spread through her body, like iced water. All she could think of was the phone, then Erin's arm over her face. Was it *her* fault? The bell started to sound louder. How could it be? What had she done?

Then she put on her trainers, pulled on her jacket and started to walk, out of the house, past David's car, still in her pyjamas. She began to pick up the pace. An ambulance, a doctor, someone had to help. She took a shortcut through a field and up the sloping hill towards the road at the top, lined with trees.

The summer breeze chilled her skin. She jogged through the muddy peatland, her mind empty of meaning or memory. The bell was ringing very loudly now, but she couldn't interpret its signal. She was just a body, a living animal body, moving its muscles to get help. David was angry with her. She didn't know why. She felt it. She would be easy to spot, exposed, like a rabbit in a field. She had to get to the trees.

When she glanced behind her, David was nowhere to be seen. And yet she expected his hand on her shoulder at any moment, shouting at her again. Her cheek still stung from where he had hit her.

After a while, it could have been ten minutes, it could have been forty-five, Joanie began to near the top of the hill, and the edge of the main road that snaked down and round to the cottage. She stood, catching her breath, and looked back, half expecting to see David racing after her.

She saw nothing except wide-open space, the twisted tree and the small garden of rosebay willowherb that sloped down towards the cliffs. David's car was still parked on the patch of gravel next to the house. Joanie looked this way and that, hugging herself, scratching at her arms. She was about to press on when she saw the figure of David below, walking backwards from the cottage towards the clifftop. He was hunched over. He was dragging something. A long shape. A woman's body. Her hair was spread out on the ground. Joanie stumbled forward. Surely he could see her from here. She hadn't reached any kind of hiding place. Just open space between the house and the trees and hills behind her. She ran forward, then stopped. She watched him from her vantage point. He dragged the body to the edge of the cliff. She looked around. There was no one, not even in the sky, not in the sea. The nearest houses were mere blobs to her left. There was the lighthouse. She was scared. The petrol station. She turned to watch David. He looked around. Then, in one quick movement, he hefted the body over the railings and off the cliff.

Joanie closed her eyes, screaming, but she still saw it. The way the body fell lifelessly over the edge, the hand still awkwardly reaching up. Then it was gone.

Instinctively, she ran as fast as she could to reach the treeline. By the time Joanie got there she leaned, panting, against a tree trunk. Her chest was tight. As she stared down towards the cliffs, the familiar bandage was wrapping itself around her ribs, sending her lungs into overdrive. She sank down on her haunches and tilted her head up to the sky. *God damn it*, she thought, her breath rapid. *Not now. You can't give up on me now.* The trees and their leafy branches were closing in. She could only sit there, as paralysed as prey, until David came to find her. Like the man who had entered her bedroom when she was fifteen.

She screwed her eyes shut and tried to picture Erin's face, the way she had talked her down from her panic attack. Night time by the East Neuk shore, a hundred years ago. *Breathe in for four and hold for seven. Got that?* The way her bangles slid down her arms.

Joanie opened one eye, her breath slowing just a little.

Time was running out, but in order to breathe, she couldn't think of David, the way he would be striding back to the house and getting into his car. She had to picture Erin. Erin alive, holding her hands, looking calmly into her eyes as Joanie's breath zigzagged between sobs. Erin teaching the meditation class. *Blue butterflies in the sand.*

Joanie's breath slowed a little more and she started to get up. She remembered the cold hand and her breath sped out of reach, like a kite in the wind. She had to leave now, had to go. She focused on the counting Erin had taught her. *One, two, three, four.* She stood up properly, open-eyed. She had to do this. Her breath was unsteady, but she was calmer. She could move. She had to stay in the moment, as Erin had taught her.

She passed through the trees and started to walk by the side of the road, peering through to see that

David's car was still parked down by the cottage. She caught sight of a figure by the cliffs. David. Hands on hips, looking around. Looking for her. She walked faster, as fast as her lungs could manage. *Breathe for four, hold for seven.*

Looking down towards David was slowing her pace. She had to push on. She had to stay focused on her body, on the road ahead. She broke into a sort of hobble-run. Her legs felt cold in her flowery pyjama pants.

As her feet pounded the verge, a voice in her head told her, *It's not your fault. It's not your fault.*

By the time the petrol station came into view, she was jogging. It was a white shape that grew bigger in the distance. If only she could have filmed him from the field. She thought of her phone, likely smashed somewhere on the rocks below, along with Erin's body. The image looped in her head as she staggered along. Erin's cold hand. *It's not your fault. Breathe for four.*

She heard the sound of an engine in the distance behind her and spun round, almost losing her balance. It was a lorry. If it had been David, he would have stopped. And then what? The petrol station was still far enough away for there to be no witnesses to whatever he would do to her. Against every instinct, she stuck out her thumb at the lorry, for a lift. The vehicle roared past her, so big she wasn't even sure the driver had seen her.

After that she picked her way back behind the trees that edged the side of the road and ran on the soft grass. She was sure that David would be able to see her from the car all the same. She wasn't sure where else he could drive to, except over sheep tracks and the coastal trail. He had to come this way sooner or later. He was angry with her.

The petrol station was closer now and an SUV was parked beside the low white building. She craned her neck back at the road behind her. Still no sign.

She picked up the pace and began to run again, straight past the petrol pumps, and pushed open the rickety door. The attendant was behind the counter, talking to someone, a bearded man in a trendy anorak, presumably the driver of the vehicle outside.

'I'm sorry to interrupt,' she said breathlessly, her voice wavering in pitch. 'I need to call the police? Don't have a phone.'

Both men looked at her in alarm. She wondered if the moustachioed man behind the counter remembered smiling at her through the window.

'What's happened?' he asked, running a hand over his chin.

'It's an emergency,' said Joanie. She didn't know what else to say. That Erin had woken up dead or that she had fallen off a cliff? Which was safer?

'My friend, she's . . .' Fear stopped her saying more, she just grabbed the phone and started dialling.

'There's been an accident,' Joanie said. 'At Fulmar's Bluff.' Should she just tell the truth? That David had kicked her phone over the edge, then thrown Erin? Was David going to tell them that she did it? Her head swirled with possibilities.

'Is this concerning the woman on the cliffs?' asked a Highland accent at the other end of the line. 'There's been another phone call. We're sending an air ambulance to the scene. The coastguard has also been notified. We'll be there shortly.'

As she put down the phone, Joanie thought of her mobile again, lying somewhere on the steep rocks. Maybe it had hit the sea. The two men by the counter were still gazing at her.

'Excuse me,' she muttered, thinking what a state she must look, as she made her way to the toilet.

Inside the pungent cubicle, she tried to catch her breath again, bent over double. *That was Erin's life*, she thought. *That was Erin's entire life*. She splashed cold water over her hot face.

As much as she preferred the safety of the cubicle's locked door, as much as she wanted to cry, she realized she had to ask to use the phone one more time, for help.

'You're Joanie?' the petrol attendant asked her, when she came back to the desk.

Had she told the emergency services her name? She couldn't be sure. The bearded SUV owner was hanging around, pretending to look at the energy drinks when she knew he was listening in.

'Yes,' she said, anxiously glancing out the window.

The petrol attendant opened his mouth to speak, but she stopped him. 'Please could I use your phone just one more time? I have to call my friend.'

'Go right ahead.'

She willed Vik's number to come back to her. It had been a joke between them, when she had gone over to his flat for pizza. Her body was shaking as she tried to punch in the numbers, hoping she had remembered correctly.

The phone started ringing. She looked out of the window at the low-lying cloud and the muted green fields. No sign yet of David's blood-red car, searching for her on the road. Maybe he was caught up with the emergency services. Telling them God knew what. The police would surely have to interview her at some point. But what would she say?

Just then she heard Vik's voice. 'This is Vikram Mohanty. Please leave a message.'

The phone went dead. She kept it to her ear. 'One moment, sorry,' she said, to the attendant, who was starting to look a little bothered, like he needed to say something. Joanie punched in the number again, but again Vik's phone went to voicemail. Of course, she thought, her heart sinking. He was working at the café. She imagined him there, serving herbal teas, with no idea of the horror that had just unfolded.

Devastated, Joanie put the phone back into its cradle. She knew she should have left a message, but she didn't know what to say to him. She didn't want to wait here for hours. No other phone numbers came to mind. She had to think, but she felt as if her brain was malfunctioning. *David*, she thought. *David had to be close.*

The petrol attendant cleared his throat. 'Your friend was in here, looking for you. Just a few minutes before you came in, it must have been. Asked us if we'd seen you.'

Joanie felt sick. 'That wasn't my friend,' she said weakly. Her thoughts spiralled as she tried to piece together a timeline. How had David's car managed to pass her on the road? It must have been when she was walking through the trees. Or was it when she was in the toilet? Surely he couldn't have seen her wandering outside.

Panic set in once again. Quickly, she turned to the SUV driver, who had moved on to browsing the toiletries.

'Can I get a lift?' she called, from the counter, her voice quavering. 'To wherever you're going? I'm sorry, but it's urgent. I can't—'

'I'm not from round here, I'm afraid,' the man said, smiling nervously while shaking his head. He must have been in his forties, his accent English. 'I wouldn't know where to—'

'No,' said Joanie, walking over to him, her eyes

wide, a manic smile on her face. David could come back at any second. 'I need to *leave*. I *really* need to get away from him. That man, who came here, looking for me,' her head snapped round to talk to the attendant, 'he was *not* my friend.'

'Oh, it was a girl,' the petrol attendant said. 'She came in here asking if I'd seen you. Said she'd come up from Fife this morning? I didn't catch her name, but she was looking for you. She had red hair. Parked a VW Beetle out there.' He gestured out of the window. 'Seemed awful worried.'

'She's gone?' Joanie croaked. It was then that the tears came. She didn't know how to stop them.

'Don't worry,' said the man, looking very worried himself now. 'I think she left her number as a matter of fact. We'll give her a call. I thought she was who you were phoning.'

That was how Joanie found herself sitting in the back room of the petrol station, watching the road outside through a security-camera screen. Only later, much later, would she feel the weight of what David had done to his girlfriend. In the moment, she thought only about the police interview she would have to give and how much truth to tell, until Cara's green car came into view.

36

Cameron, 1 January 2024

I arrived at two p.m. on New Year's Day, as the message had demanded. Bleary-eyed, I couldn't even find a parking space close to the South Sands. I was still thinking of the roast pork I had made for the family. I had had to wolf it down and make excuses to leave. It was giving me indigestion. I felt self-conscious wearing one of my dad's old jackets, as Mia still had mine. She said she would meet me in town later. I hadn't told her about the last Christmas card. I should have remembered the place would be packed. As I walked to the top of the beach, I saw a homemade banner, threatening to fly off down to the rocks. It advertised the St Rule Loony Dook, the New Year's Day tradition, in large, painted letters. I had completely forgotten. This wasn't a student thing, per se, but something the whole town did each year.

How on earth was I meant to find someone among this crowd? Hundreds of people scattered across the sand, in swimwear, towels and Dryrobes, waiting to run into the icy sea. I could see some people were raising money for charity. Many were in groups of friends, marked by matching outfits. Everyone was talking and sipping from Thermos flasks. Some were wearing swimming caps, others woolly hats and gloves.

How would this person even begin to find me in the crowd? They had sent me on a wild-goose chase. I should have known better.

I turned around and the hair stood up on the back of my neck. There, a few yards behind me, Tatey was texting on his phone. I did a double-take. This couldn't be a coincidence. The bastard.

I looked round and spotted Cara's red hair in the crowd nearby. She was wearing a puffer jacket and jeans. Someone planning to stay on dry land. I wasn't sure whom I had been expecting, but it wasn't Cara. I started walking in the other direction, dodging swimmers here and there, until I saw someone else in the distance, the man I had last seen on the beach. I spun round to walk back the way I had come, and then I saw her. It was unmistakably her.

Joanie.

She was standing in a parka, facing towards me now, away from the sea. She was older; of course she was.

A wave of relief washed over me, then something

else, a pang of sheepishness and puzzlement as she started to walk towards me, straight-faced. All the times I had watched her in my mind's eye, she was still the teenage girl from school: her light-brown hair was long and soft in my imagination. She was always smiling at me, teasing me. There had been some hint that there might be something more between us. I had been so worried I might never see her again. Now here she was and I realized I was meeting a stranger, maybe even someone who had scared me, made me feel unsafe.

I was relieved to see her; of course I was. Yet, it would be an understatement to say that this wasn't the reunion I had hoped for or, I admit, dreamed about. I felt at a loss for words.

Her clothes bore no resemblance to the style I remembered. Jeans and trainers. Bog standard. Nondescript. She was still beautiful, though. There was no doubting it.

'I heard you were asking after me.' Her voice was guarded. Not the voice from my memory. It was foolish the way I had imagined her, like Snow White preserved in a glass coffin.

'I'm sorry.' That was all I could think of saying. I smiled, hoping that would put her at ease, make up for something. 'Did you send me those Christmas cards?' I asked tentatively.

She nodded, like she was admitting to sending me your average season's greetings. 'I didn't want to see you,' she said evenly. 'Elise, my sister? She said you came to my mum's door.'

I remembered seeing someone run up the stairs behind her stepfather, as I stood there. Joanie's teenage doppelgänger.

'You've got some cheek,' Joanie continued coolly. 'Why couldn't you leave them alone?'

'Um. Ouch.' I shouldn't have said that. I knew it as soon as I said it. Something was very wrong.

She raised her eyebrows, while the rest of her face remained unchanged. I hoped she would fill the silence, but she stayed looking at me expectantly.

There must have been some kind of grave misunderstanding, for her to act this way towards me. It was possible that the intervening years had loosened her grip on reality.

'Look,' I said, wondering how best to put it, 'this will sound silly, now we've met, but I've actually been worried about you. No one I knew had heard anything about you for years. It was so strange. I was asking people about you, simply because I wanted to check you were OK. I don't think I did anything wrong.'

Her green eyes softened a little. 'That was thoughtful of you. I appreciate it, but I can explain. I keep a low profile. I don't do social media.'

She shrugged, expressionless. 'It's important that no one knows where I am.'

'Well,' I said, jumping in, 'OK, I understand. It's

great to see you.' Another understatement. 'Did you . . . put that card in my pocket?'

She shook her head. I thought back to how tightly Tatey had hugged me.

A loud bang went off and she jumped out of her skin. A starter's pistol. The whole beach began running away from us, whooping and screaming into the sea.

We couldn't end on this note. This was nothing like I had imagined and I had no idea why. 'I thought you might be dead,' I said.

She took a deep breath, then came at me with a torrent of words. 'Aside from you, that was the single most *terrifying* time in my life. The year we left school. Something awful happened. Really awful. I can't go into the details, but I am asking you to leave me and my family alone, Cameron. Believe me when I say you don't know what the consequences could be. There is someone out there, someone dangerous, and I don't want him to know a thing about me.' She was clearly distraught, but there was something else.

'Sorry, did you say *aside from you*?' I asked. '*I* terrified you?'

'Yes.'

She clearly wasn't well. 'OK,' I said. 'I'm picking up you're maybe not the most pleased to see me and I guess I'll respect that.'

Joanie's face changed to one of derision. 'Sorry,

you'll *respect that*? I know what you did. Now, anyway.'

I couldn't believe this. 'Know what I did?'

'Tatey told me, a few years ago. He's actually been a good friend through all this. He helped me out of a really tough situation. He told me you were here, actually. Trying to find out where I was.'

'Is that such a bad thing?' I asked. I shook my head in the silence that followed. Tatey. All that talk about *me* being a dark horse. I ran my hand through my hair. 'I don't know what you're talking about, I'm sorry.'

'No. You don't get to do that. Don't *pretend* you don't know. My house. I know you came into my house. That night.' She looked at me intently.

A cold dread spread through me.

I began to tell her that I had no idea what she was talking about, but my voice quavered. I couldn't do it. 'I'm so sorry,' I said. '*I'm so, so sorry.*'

Her eyes darted over my face. 'How could you? It really fucked me up.'

She was talking about something years and years ago, when we were at school and she and Tatey and I would play tricks on each other. It was a stupid prank that went wrong. Something I thought she didn't know about. 'All I can say is that we were in S4. I was a fifteen-year-old boy,' I replied. My heart was starting to beat faster.

'I know, I was a *fifteen-year-old girl*, Cameron.

I can't tell you how *terrified* I was. I thought I was going to die.'

'You were *in the house*?' This was horrifying. 'I saw your car drive away. It wasn't only me, you know. Tatey was going to do it, then chickened out.'

'I was in the house. I think you knew that. What the fuck were you doing? Breaking in?' She looked so angry. She could hardly spit the words out.

We had flipped into a parallel universe where everything was awful. 'It was stupid. I'm sorry,' I said, my voice small. This wasn't what I'd come to talk about.

'Why? Why would you even do that?' She looked around, exasperated, tears in the corners of her eyes.

'Because. Because it was a prank . . .' It sounded so stupid to say it now.

'If you liked me, why did you scare the *shit* out of me? Creeping about in my house. I thought that you were a burglar. I mean, what you did was *a crime*. Were you trying to steal something? Do something to me?'

'No. I wasn't a burglar. I was just a boy. I didn't even know you were there. Really. I'm sorry. I genuinely am so sorry.' I could taste acid at the back of my throat.

Years before Joanie left the party at Boar's Raik, in the annals of Hallow's Hill Secondary School, in the mists of time at St Rule, there had been an idea for a prank. A stupid plan. It had started when Tatey and I had overheard Joanie talking to her friend in class about how a back window at home wouldn't shut properly.

We had hatched the idea to go into her creepy house and place something there. It was just before Tatey had been kicked out of the choir for wearing that damn Viking helmet. He had suggested that I go into her house and place it on the dining-table. Would her mother even notice something new in there? Surely she would. We had agreed to do it together and then he said no: he was having second thoughts. It wasn't a good prank.

After all the rumours about Joanie's mum being a hoarder, it played on my mind. One Saturday evening weeks later, after playing video games at Graham's, I saw Joanie's car driving out of the cul-de-sac, with the family inside. The house was dark. It seemed, at the time, like an opportunity that was too good to miss. Thankfully, there was no security light as I snuck round the back, but the next door's dog started barking. My heart hammered in my chest. I didn't have the Viking helmet. I thought about leaving the baseball cap I was wearing.

I hoisted myself up and wedged the window open, then squeezed through. I was in an unfamiliar space, but the layout of the house was similar to Graham's so I had some sense of where I was meant to be going. I wasn't quite expecting how dark and chock-a-block everything was inside. It was hard to move about without knocking anything over. It smelt awful, too. I didn't know how they could live like that. As soon as I was inside, I felt terrible. And yet.

The stairs creaked as I walked up towards the bedrooms. I don't know why, but I did. I kept telling myself there was no way the family would come home; I had to calm down. Then I stepped on something sharp. I picked it up. A tiny plastic rabbit. A child's toy. I realized how foolish it all was and ran back down the stairs, then climbed out of the window. And that had been that.

At least, that was the story I had told myself all these years.

Whenever I had had an intrusive thought about that shameful night, I'd told myself that I had never really done anything wrong and it didn't bear thinking about. I hadn't stolen anything and the house had been empty. No harm, no foul.

Yet now another memory surfaced, an uncertain one. If I was honest with myself, which was very difficult, I had left the house not because of stepping on something but because I had heard a noise in the dark. That was why I had gone upstairs. I'd wondered if Joanie was up there. I told myself later that my mind had played tricks on me, but I had been sure I'd heard a gasp and a creak in the pitch black. She had been in the house. If I was *really* honest with myself, I did sort of know that. Had I opened a door? A bedroom door? I had been startled by a black shape, a cat bolting out of the bedroom. Had there been a scream, or was it my imagination? Either way, I had felt a deep sense of shame and exited as fast as I could, tripping over things, making too much noise.

Nearly fifteen years later, there was no way I could explain all of this. The mortification must have been visible on my face. I was sure she could see it. It had been such a long journey to find her. I couldn't bear the thought that she might have been in danger. Somehow it would have been my fault. Shame had lingered in my bones. I had always wondered if the police would find me. Maybe part of my subconscious thought that if I could be sure she was OK it would make up for what I had done.

She was looking at me steadily. 'I would really like to be left alone, Cameron. I hope you understand that.'

'Yes,' I said. 'I understand.'

Her expression looked either angry or scared, I couldn't tell which.

The man in the baseball cap now came into view, the one who had been watching me on the beach. 'You OK, love?' he asked Joanie.

Was he the one who had written the cards?

'Maybe some day,' I said, facing Joanie, ignoring him, 'we can be friends again.'

'Yes,' she nodded, deadpan. 'Maybe. I just wanted to give you a scare first.'

I stood in the sand as the pair of them left, walking up the beach, to the car park, amid the rush of people who were shivering in towels. Tatey and Cara were nowhere to be seen. I took out my phone to tell Mia I was on my way into town. I didn't know how to explain it, but I doubted I knew the full truth about Joanie. I doubted it more than I ever had before.

37

Joanie, 2 January 2024

NO TO NIGHTSHADE

This final blog post is to say thank you for your support over the years. Now, as the new year starts, for the first time in my life, I go forward with optimism. I want to share with you my explosive news. Those of you who have known me these past five years as No to Nightshade will have noticed that I have kept my origins and my relationship to David vague. You may come to know my real name in the press, but for now I will keep it under wraps. We have finally gathered enough evidence to bring a case against David Henderson. For this reason, it is time for this website to close.

Joanie submitted her final update in the plush anonymity of her hotel room. From the large window, overlooking a golf course, she could just make out the skyline of St Rule.

'It's done,' she said to Vik, who was packing their suitcase. He walked over silently and hugged her, kissed the back of her head as she stayed seated at the desk. He had seen how much this had taken from her, over the years, from both of them, while David's influence in academic circles had grown.

Joanie would never forget the day in September, ten years ago, when the police had knocked at her door. Her mother's stricken face as she had ushered them into their overstuffed living room. Joanie's legs had still ached from the car journey home earlier that day. The police interview was something that she played over in her mind to this day. The strange relief when she had realized that they were not there to arrest her, but to hear her version of events. She had told them that day, and then later, as part of the Fatal Accident Inquiry, that Erin had spoken to her shortly after she had experimented with henbane. That Joanie had not seen Erin take it, because she had been talking to David. Then Joanie had said she had gone to bed. It had felt too easy to omit the conversation she had overheard. She had been too scared to say that she too had been under the plant's influence. Instead, she said that Erin had been absent from the cottage when Joanie had woken up. That she had gone to meet Cara that morning, unaware of what had happened to Erin. Her testimony had made her feel sick, but telling the truth had felt impossible at the time. At eighteen years old, she had been a coward, hoping to avoid the wrath of David, but guilt had since twisted and calcified inside her.

Perhaps it had been a terrible, accidental overdose, Joanie had tried to tell herself, whenever she had lain awake at night. At the same time, she had no doubt that David could kill her if he wanted to.

Without knowing it, her witness statement had been close enough to David's that the Sheriff had ruled Erin's death a tragic accident, under the influence of a hallucinogenic poison she hadn't understood. In the intervening years, one or two articles had been written about David's work and his relationship with Erin, but he had cast himself as grief-stricken. Erin's death, he had said, had increased his determination to widen the understanding of this mysterious plant. He had raised eyebrows, certainly, but found dedicated acolytes too.

Before Joanie and Vik's trip home to Bologna, there was one more thing left to do. It was time for them to make their yearly visit to strew sage and apple mint on Erin's final resting place, at the cemetery near Thurso. It was never an easy trip. And on the way up, whenever they passed the sign for Aberdeen, Joanie thought of the university place she had given up on when her world had been shaken to the core. For the past decade, the shame she had felt, about not telling the full truth to the police, had at times been almost too much to bear. Joanie's phone had never been recovered among the jagged rocks that dropped two hundred feet into the sea. About a year after Erin's death, she had begun to realize the full extent of David's manipulation, but that hadn't stopped her feeling terrified of him. Sometimes anonymous threatening messages would turn up in unexpected places. Her email inbox. Even the university library pigeon hole in Bologna. She knew they were from him, but had no way of proving it. After five years of living abroad with Vik, working at the Biblioteca Universitaria, she had started the website, researching his practices and collecting testimonies against him from others he had harmed. Little by little, she had started to feel stronger. No one was ever going to make her feel that powerless again.

She had said goodbye to her mum and sister earlier that morning, in the hotel grounds. She visited them and her father for Christmas and the summer holidays, mostly to see Elise. She often stayed at the hotel, which was big enough to wander about and had security guards who made her feel safe. She avoided the town, for the most part, and there was no way she could stay in her old bedroom, even if she had wanted to. In her absence, her mother had filled the space with boxes and bags of indeterminate junk. *Ephemera.*

BLUFF

Before Joanie closed her laptop, she reread two emails, one from her lawyer and one from Chloë. A year ago, Joanie had started talking to Cameron's former girlfriend-turned-journalist, after seeing an article she had written investigating a religious scandal. It was Chloë who had gathered evidence with her, to write a forthcoming exposé. They had enough witness testimonies now to expose David's faked research and coercive behaviour. Chloë had helped her find the right words to talk about it. Joanie stood up and looked out of the hotel-room window. The winter sun glared down on the steepled silhouette of St Rule. It was time to come forward with her story. She was no longer afraid of the dark.

Author's Note

While the majority of places in *Bluff* are fictional, they have real-life inspiration in the form of St Andrews (St Rule), Boarhills (Boar's Raik), Kingsbarns (Monypenny), Olrig (Olrich) and the Isle of May (Maeyar, which sits in a slightly different location to its real-life counterpart). St Adrian of May was the inspiration behind his heathen parallel, Aiden of Maeyar. Unlike Aiden, St Adrian was murdered by Danish invaders in 875, becoming a Christian martyr.

I was inspired to write about the Viking use of henbane after reading ethnobotanist Karsten Fatur's paper 'Sagas of the Solanaceae: speculative ethnobotanical perspectives on the Norse berserkers', published in the *Journal of Ethnopharmacology* in 2019.

Acknowledgements

A big thank-you to my talented, kind and insightful editors at Doubleday, Sarah Adams, Lara Stevenson and Bobby Mostyn-Owen, and to my agent Alice Lutyens, for her boundless enthusiasm and sage advice. Thank you to Billy Lindon, for their brilliant editorial brain at a time when it was most needed. Thank you to Tom Shepherd for helping with research early in the writing process; to The Bowies for their knowledge of Caithness; to my lovely Fife friends; to my wonderful colleagues at The Novelry; to Livia Franchini and Michael Marshall for their academic insight (any mistakes are my own); to my Friday writing buddies, Anbara, Kirsty, Imogen, and the support of WwF. Thank you to my awesome pals G Bowie and Nick Cole-Hamilton for taking the time to read through drafts and talk through ideas. Thank you to my father Stephen for reading so carefully. Thank you to my mother Annie and sister Lottie for cheering me on. Thank you to Youcef for being the sunshine in my life. Yassine, I am eternally grateful for your enduring support, in ways big and small; your patience and love mean the world.

Francine Toon's debut novel, *Pine*, was a *Sunday Times* bestseller and number one *Times* bestseller. It won the 2020 McIlvanney Prize, was shortlisted for the Bloody Scotland Debut Prize and longlisted for the Highland Book Prize and the Deborah Rogers Foundation Writers Award.

Her poetry, written as Francine Elena, has appeared in the *Sunday Times*, *The Best British Poetry* 2013 and 2015 anthologies, and *Poetry London*, among other places. Her short story 'Ghost Kitchen' was published in the anthology *Of The Flesh*.